LABYRINTH
THE NOVELIZATION

Published by
ARCHAIA™

LABYRINTH
THE NOVELIZATION

Based on the Jim Henson film

Adapted by
A. C. H. SMITH

Illustrations by
BRIAN FROUD

Jim Henson's LABYRINTH™

Labyrinth is based on the movie produced by Jim Henson, George Lucas, and Eric Rattray, directed by Jim Henson, with George Lucas as Executive Producer, David Lazer as Executive Supervising Producer, screenplay by Terry Jones, and conceptual design by Brian Froud. The screenplay by Terry Jones is based on the story by Jim Henson and Dennis Lee. With a special thanks to Laura Phillips.

Type Layout by **Scott Newman**
Cover Design by **Faceout Studio**
Additional Design by **Emi Yonemura Brown**
The Jim Henson Company Archivist, **Karen Falk**
Assistant Editor, Archaia Edition, **Cameron Chittock**
Editors, Archaia Edition, **Stephen Christy & Rebecca Taylor**

ARCHAIA™ | **Jim Henson**
THE JIM HENSON COMPANY

Special Thanks to Brian Henson, Lisa Henson, Jim Formanek, Nicole Goldman, Maryanne Pittman, Carla Dellavedova, Justin Hilden, Karen Falk, and the entire Jim Henson Company team, Forrest Lighthart, Charles Brock, Torrey Sharp, Kelly Vlach, and the entire Faceout Studio team.

BOOM! Studios, 6920 Melrose Ave., Los Angeles, CA, 90038.
Printed in China. Sixth Printing.

ISBN: 978-1-68415-299-5, eISBN: 978-1-64144-152-0

CONTENTS

LABYRINTH™
THE NOVELIZATION

CHAPTER I
THE WHITE OWL

Nobody saw the owl, white in the moonlight, black against the stars, nobody heard him as he glided over on silent wings of velvet. The owl saw and heard everything.

He settled in a tree, his claws hooked on a branch, and he stared at the girl in the glade below. The wind moaned, rocking the branch, scudding low clouds across the evening sky. It lifted the hair of the girl. The owl was watching her, with his round, dark eyes.

The girl moved slowly from the trees toward the middle of the glade, where a pool glimmered. She was concentrating. Each deliberate step took her nearer to her purpose. Her hands were open, and held slightly in front of her. The wind sighed again in the trees. It blew her cloak tightly against her slender figure, and rustled her hair around her wide-eyed face. Her lips were parted.

"Give me the child," Sarah said, in a voice that was low, but firm with the courage her quest needed. She halted, her hands still held out. "Give me the child," she repeated. "Through dangers untold and hardships unnumbered, I have fought my way here to the castle beyond the Goblin City, to take back the child you have stolen." She bit her lip and continued, "For my will is as strong as yours… and my kingdom as great…."

She closed her eyes tightly. Thunder rumbled. The owl blinked, once.

"My will is as strong as yours." Sarah spoke with even more intensity now. "And my kingdom as great…" She frowned, and her shoulders dropped.

"Oh damn," she muttered.

Reaching under her cloak, she brought out a book. Its title was *The Labyrinth*. Holding the book up before her, she read aloud from it. In the fading light, it was not easy to make out the words. "You have no power over me…."

She got no further. Another clap of thunder, nearer this time, made her jump. It also alarmed a big, shaggy sheepdog, who had not minded sitting by the pool and being admonished by Sarah, but who now decided that it was time to go home, and said so with several sharp barks.

Sarah held her cloak around her. It did not give her much warmth, being no more than an old curtain, cut down, and fastened at the neck by a glass brooch. She ignored Merlin, the sheepdog, while concentrating on learning the speech in the book. "You have no power over me," she whispered. She closed her eyes again and repeated the phrase several times.

A clock above the little pavilion in the park chimed seven times and penetrated Sarah's concentration. She stared at Merlin. "Oh, no," she said. "I don't believe it. That was *seven*, wasn't it?"

Merlin stood up and shook himself, sensing that some more interesting action was due. Sarah turned and ran. Merlin followed. The thunderclouds splattered them both with large drops of rain.

The owl had watched it all. When Sarah and Merlin left the park, he sat still on his branch, in no hurry to follow them. This was his time of day. He knew what he wanted. An owl is born with all his questions answered.

All the way down the street, which was lined on both sides with privet-hedged Victorian houses similar to her own, Sarah was muttering to herself, "It's not fair, it's not fair. " The mutter had turned to a gasp by the time she came within sight of her home. Merlin, having bounded along with her on the shaggy paws, was wheezing, too. His mistress, who normally moved at a gentle, dreamy pace, had this odd habit of liking to sprint home from the park in the evening. Perhaps that owl had something to do with it. Merlin was not sure. He didn't like the owl, he knew that.

"It's not *fair*." Sarah was close to sobbing. The world at large was not fair, hardly ever, but in particular her stepmother was ruthlessly not fair to her. There she stood now, in the front doorway of the house, all dressed up in that frightful, dark blue evening gown of hers, the fur coat left open to reveal the low cut of the neckline, the awful necklace vulgarly winking above her freckled breast, and—wouldn't you know?—she was looking at her watch. Not just looking at it but staring at it, to make good and sure that Sarah would feel guilty before she was accused, again.

As Sarah came to a halt on the path in the front garden, she could hear her baby brother, Toby, bawling inside the house. He was her half brother really, but she did not call him that, not since her school friend Alice had asked, "What's the other half of him, then?" and Sarah had been unable to think of an answer. "Half nothing-to-do-with-me." That was no good. It wasn't true, either. Sometimes she felt fiercely protective of Toby, wanted to dress him up and carry him in her arms and take him away from all this, to a better place, a fairer world, an island somewhere, perhaps. At other times—and this was one—she hated Toby, who had twice as many parents in attendance on him as she had. When she hated Toby, it frightened her, because it led her into thinking about how she could hurt him. There must be something wrong with me, she would reflect, that I can even think of hurting someone I dote upon; or is it that there is something wrong in doting upon someone I hate? She wished she had a friend who would understand the dilemma, and maybe explain it to her, but there was no one. Her friends at school would think her a witch if she even mentioned the idea of hurting Toby, and as for her father, it would frighten him even more than it frightened Sarah herself. So she kept the perplexity well hidden.

Sarah stood before her stepmother and deliberately held her head high. "I'm sorry," she said, in a bored voice, to show that she wasn't sorry at all, and anyway it was unnecessary to make a thing out of it.

"Well," her stepmother told her, "don't stand out there in the rain. Come on." She stood aside, to make room for Sarah to pass her in the doorway, and she glanced again at her wristwatch.

Sarah made a point of never touching her stepmother, not even brushing against her clothes. She edged inside close to the door frame. Merlin started to follow her.

"Not the dog," her stepmother said.

"But it's pouring."

Her stepmother wagged her finger at Merlin, twice. "In the garage, you," she commanded. "Go on."

Merlin dropped his head and loped around the side of the house. Sarah watched him go and bit her lip. Why, she wondered for the trillionth time, does my stepmother always have to put on this performance when they go out in the evening? It was so *hammy*—that was one of Sarah's favorite words, since she had heard her mother's costar, Jeremy, use it to put down another actor in the play they were doing—such a *ragbag of over-the-top clichés*. She remembered how Jeremy had sounded French when he said *clichés*, thrilling her with his sophistication. Why couldn't her stepmother find *a new way into the part*? Oh, she loved the way in which Jeremy talked about other actors. She was determined to become an actress herself, so that she could talk like that all the time. Her father seldom talked at all about people at his office, and when he did it was dreary in comparison.

Her stepmother closed the front door, looked at her watch once more, took a deep breath, and started one of her clichéd speeches. "Sarah, you're an hour late...."

Sarah opened her mouth, but her stepmother cut her off, with a little, humorless smile.

"Please let me finish, Sarah. Your father and I go out very rarely—"

"You go out every weekend," Sarah interrupted rapidly.

Her stepmother ignored that. "—and I ask you to baby-sit only if it won't interfere with your plans."

"How would you know?" Sarah had half turned away, so as not to flatter her stepmother with her attention, and was busy with putting her book on the hall stand, unclipping her brooch, and folding the cloak over her arm. "You don't know what my plans are. You don't ask me." She glanced at her own face in the mirror of the hall stand, checking that her expression was cool and poised, not *over the top*. She liked the clothes she was wearing: a cream-colored shirt with full sleeves, a brocaded waistcoat loosely over the shirt, blue jeans, and a leather belt. She turned even farther away from her stepmother, to check on how her shirt hung from her breasts down to her waist. She tucked it in a little at the belt, to make it tighter.

Her stepmother was watching her coldly. "I am assuming you

would tell me if you had a date. I would *like* it if you had a date. A fifteen-year-old girl *should* have dates."

Well, Sarah was thinking, if I did have a date you are the *last* person I would tell. What a hammy—no, *tacky*—view of life you do have. She smiled grimly to herself. Perhaps I will have a date, she thought, perhaps I will, but you will *not* like it, not one bit, when you see who's dating me. I doubt you will see him. All you will know about it is hearing the front door shut behind me, and you will sneak to the window, as you always do, and poke your nose between those horrid phony-lace curtains you put up there, and you will see the taillights of a wicked dove-gray limousine vanishing around the corner. And after that, you will keep seeing pictures in the magazines of the two of us together in Bermuda, and St. Tropez, and Benares. And there will be nothing at all you can possibly do about it, for all your firm views on bedtimes and developmental psychology and my duties and rolling up the toothpaste tube from the bottom. Oh, stepmother, are you going to be sorry when you read in *Vogue* about the cosmic cash that Hollywood producers are offering us for—

Sarah's father came down the stairs into the hall. In his arms he was carrying Toby, clad in red-and-white-striped pajamas. He patted the baby's back. "Oh, Sarah," he said mildly, "you're here at last. We were worried about you."

"Oh, leave me alone!" Afraid that she might be close to tears, Sarah gave them no chance to reason with her. She ran upstairs. They were always so reasonable, particularly her father, so long-suffering and mild with her, so utterly convinced that they were always obviously in the right, and that it was only a matter of time before she consented to do as they wished. Why did her father always take that woman's side? Her mother never wore that look of pained tolerance. She was a woman who could shout and laugh and hug you and slap you all within a minute or two. When she and Sarah had a quarrel, it was an explosion. Five minutes later, it was forgotten.

In the hallway, her stepmother had sat down, still in her fur coat. Wearily, she was saying, "I don't know *what* to do anymore. She treats me like the wicked stepmother in a fairy tale, no matter what I say. I have tried, Robert."

"Well…" Sarah's father patted Toby thoughtfully. "It *is* hard to have your mother walk out on you at that age. At any age, I suppose."

"That's what you always say. And of course you're right. But will she never change?"

Holding Toby in one arm, Robert patted his wife on the shoulder. "I'll go and talk to her."

Thunder rumbled again. A squall of raindrops clattered on the windows.

Sarah was in her room. It was the only safe place in the world. She made a point of going all around it each day, checking that everything was just where it had been and should be. Although her stepmother seldom came in there, except to deliver some ironed clothes or to give Sarah a message, she was not to be trusted. It would be typical of her to take it into her head to dust the room, even though Sarah made sure that it was kept clean, and then she would be bound to move things around and not put them back where they belonged. It was essential to ward off that disturbing spirit.

All the books had to remain in their proper positions, in alphabetical order by author and, within each author's group, in order of acquisition. Other shelves were filled with toys and dolls, and they were positioned according to affinities known only to Sarah. The curtains had to hang exactly so that, when Sarah was lying on her bed, they symmetrically framed the second poplar tree in a line that she could see from the window. The wastepaper basket stood so that its base jut touched the edge of one particular block on the parquet floor. It would be unsafe if these things were not so. Once let disorder set in, and the room would never be familiar again. People talked about how upsetting it was to be burgled, and Sarah knew just how it must feel, as though some uncaring stranger were fooling around with your most precious soul. The woman who came in to clean three times a week knew that she was never to do anything to this room. Sarah looked after everything in there herself. She had learned how to fix electric plugs, and tighten screws, and hang pictures, so that her father should have no need to come in except to speak to her.

Sarah was now standing in the middle of her room. Her eyes were red. She sniffled, and chewed her lower lip. Then she walked over to her dressing table and gazed at a framed photograph. Her father and mother, and herself, aged ten, gazed back at her. Her parents' smiles were confident. Her own face in the photograph was, she thought, slightly over the top, grinning too keenly.

All around the room, other eyes watched. Photographs and posters displayed her mother in various costumes, for various parts. Clippings from *Variety* were taped to the mirror of the dressing table, praising her mother's performances or announcing others she would give. On the wall beside the bed was pinned a poster advertising her latest play; in the picture, Sarah's mother and her costar, Jeremy, were cheek to cheek, their arms around each other, smiling confidently. The photographer had lit the pair beautifully, showing her to be so pretty, he so handsome, with his blond hair and a golden chain around his neck. Beneath the picture was a quote from one of the theater critics: "I have seldom felt such warmth irradiating an audience." The poster was signed, with large flourishing signatures: "For Darling Sarah, with all my love, Mom," and, in a different hand, "All Good Wishes, Sarah—Jeremy." Near the poster were more press clippings, from different newspapers, arranged in chronological order. In them, the two stars could be seen dining together in restaurants, drinking together at parties, and laughing together in a little rowboat. The texts were all on the theme of "Romancing on and off the stage."

Still sniffling from time to time, Sarah went to the small table beside her bed and picked up the music box her mother had given her for her fifteenth birthday. The memory of that gorgeous day was still vivid. A taxi had been sent for her in the morning, but instead of going to her mother's place it had taken her along the waterfront to where Jeremy and her mother were waiting in Jeremy's old black Mercedes. They went out into the country for lunch beside a swimming pool at some club where Jeremy was a member and the waiters spoke French, and later, in the pool, Jeremy had clowned around, pretending to drown, to such effect that an elderly man had rug the alarm bell. They had giggled in the car all the way back to town. At her mother's place, Sarah was given Jeremy's present, an evening gown in pale blue. She wore it to go with them to a new musical that evening, and afterward to supper, in a dimly lit restaurant. Jeremy was wickedly funny about every member of the cast they had seen in the musical. Sarah's mother had pretended to disapprove of his scandalous gossip, but that had only made Sarah and Jeremy laugh more uncontrollably, and soon all three of them had tears in their eyes. Jeremy had danced with Sarah, smiling down at her. He kidded her that a flashbulb meant that they'd be all over the gossip columns next morning, and all the way home he drove fast, to shake off the photographers, he claimed, grinning. As they said good night, her mother gave Sarah a little parcel, wrapped in silver paper and tied with a pale blue bow. Back in her room, Sarah had unwrapped it, and found the music box.

The tune of "Greensleeves" tinkled, and a little dancer in a frilly pink dress twirled pirouettes. Sarah watched it reverently, until it became slow and jerky in motion. Then she put it down, and quietly recited from a poem she had studied in her English class:

> "O body swayed to music, O brightening glance,
> How can we know the dancer from the dance?"

It was so easy to learn poetry by heart. She never had any difficulty in remembering those lines, whenever she opened the music box. In fact, she reflected, it's easier to remember them than to forget them. So why was she having such trouble in learning the speech from *The Labyrinth*? It was only a game she was playing. No one was waiting for her to rehearse it, no audience, except Merlin, would judge her performance of it. It should have been a piece of cake. She frowned. How could she ever hope to go on the stage if she could not remember one speech?

She tried again. "Through dangers untold and hardships unnumbered, I have fought my way here to the castle beyond the Goblin City, to take back the child you have stolen…." She paused, her eyes on the poster of her mother in Jeremy's arms, and decided it would help her performance if she prepared for it. If you're going to get into a part, her mother had told her, you've got to have the right prop. Costume and makeup and wigs—they were more for the actor's benefit than for the audience's. They helped you escape from your own life and *find your way into the part*, as Jeremy said. And after each show, you take it all off, and you've wiped the slate clean. Every day was a fresh start. You could invent yourself again. Sarah took a lipstick from the drawer in her dressing table, put a little on her lips, and rolled them together, as her mother did. Her face close to the mirror, she applied a little more to the corners of her mouth.

There was a tapping on her door, and her father's voice came from outside. "Sarah? Can I talk to you?"

Still looking in the mirror, she replied, "There's nothing to talk about."

She waited. He would not come in unless she invited him. She imagined him standing there, frowning, rubbing his forehead, trying to think what he ought to say next, something firm enough to please that woman but amicable enough to reassure his daughter.

"You'd better hurry," Sarah said, "if you want to make the show."

"Toby's had his supper," her father's voice said, "and he's in bed now. If you could just make sure he goes to sleep all right, we'll be back around midnight."

Again, a pause, then the sound of footsteps walking away, with a slowness measured to express a blend of concern and resignation. He had done all that could be expected of him.

Sarah turned from the mirror and stared accusingly at the closed door. "You really wanted to talk to me, didn't you?" she murmured. "Practically broke down the door." Once upon a time, he would not have gone out without giving her a kiss. She sniffled. Things had certainly changed in this house.

She put the lipstick in her pocket and wiped her lips with a tissue. As she went to throw it in the wastepaper basket, something caught her eye. More exactly, something that was not there caught her eye. Launcelot was not there.

Rapidly, she rummaged through her shelf of toys and dolls and cuddly things, dogs and monkeys and soldiers and clowns, though she knew it would be fruitless. If the teddy bear were there at all, he would have been in his appointed place. He had gone. The order of the room had been violated. Sarah's cheeks were hot.

Someone's been in my room, she thought. I hate her.

Outside, the taxi was pulling away. Sarah heard it and ran to the window.

"I *hate* you," she screamed.

No one heard her save Merlin, and he could do no more than he was doing already, which was to bark loudly, in the garage.

She knew where she would find Launcelot. Toby already had everything that his baby heart could desire, had so much more than Sarah had ever had; yet more was given to him, every day, without question. She stormed into the nursery. The teddy bear was spread-eagled on the carpet, just tossed away, like that. Sarah picked Launcelot up and clutched him to her. Toby, full of warm milk, had been almost asleep in his crib. Sarah's entrance aroused him.

She glared at the baby. "I hate her. I hate you."

Toby started to cry. Sarah shuddered, and held Launcelot still more tightly.

"Oh," she wailed. "Oh, someone… save me. Take me away from this awful place."

Toby was howling now. His face was red. Sarah was wailing, Merlin was barking outside. The storm delivered a lightning flash and clap of thunder directly above the house. It rattled the windows in their frames. Teacups danced in the kitchen cupboard.

"Someone save me," Sarah begged.

"Listen!" said a goblin, one eye opened.

All around him, on top of him, beneath him, the nest of goblins stirred sleepily. Another eye opened, and another, and another, all crazed eyes, red and staring. Some of the goblins had horns, and some had pointed teeth, some had fingers like claws; some were dressed in scraps of armor, a helmet, a gorget, but all of them had scaly feet, and all had baleful eyes. Higgledy-piggledy in a heap they slept, in their dirty chamber at the castle of the Goblin King. Their eyes went on opening, and their ears pricked up.

"All right, hush now, shush." Sarah was trying to calm herself down as much as her baby brother. "What do you want? Hmm? Do you want a story? All right." With barely a moment's thought, she picked up the thread of *The Labyrinth.* "Once upon a time there was a beautiful young woman whose stepmother always made her stay with the baby. The baby was a spoiled child who wanted everything for himself, and the young woman was practically a slave girl. But what no one knew was this: the King of the Goblins had fallen in love with her, and given her certain powers."

In the castle, the goblins' eyes opened very wide. They were all attention.

The lightning and thunder crashed again, but both Sarah and Toby had become quieter. "One night," Sarah continued, "when the baby had been particularly nasty, the girl called on the goblins to help her. And they said to her, 'Say your right words, and we'll take the baby away to the Goblin City, and then you'll be free.' Those were their words to her."

The goblins nodded enthusiastically.

Toby was nearly asleep again, with only a light protest remaining on his breath. Sarah, enjoying her own invention, leaned closer to him, over the side of the crib. She was holding her audience in her spell. Launcelot was in her arms.

"But the girl knew," she went on, "that the King of the Goblins would keep the baby in his castle forever and ever, and he would turn the baby into a goblin. And so she suffered in silence, through many a long month… until one night, worn out by a day of slaving at housework, and hurt beyond measure by the harsh, ungrateful words of her stepmother, she could bear it no longer."

By now, Sarah was leaning so close to Toby that she was whispering into his little pink ear. Suddenly he turned over in his crib and stared into her eyes, only a couple of inches away. There was a moment of silence. Then Toby opened his mouth, and began to howl loudly and insistently.

"Oh!" Sarah snorted in disgust, standing up straight again.

The thunder rolled, and Merlin gave it all he had.

Sarah sighed, frowned, shrugged, and decided there was no way around it. She picked Toby up and walked around the room, jogging him in her arms, together with Launcelot. The small bedside light threw their shadows on the wall, huge and flickering. "All right," she said, "all right. Come on, now. Rock-a-bye baby, and all that stuff. Come on, Toby, knock it off."

Toby wasn't going to knock it off just for being jogged. He felt he had a serious grievance to express.

"Toby," his sister said sternly, "be quiet, will you? Please? Or—" Her voice lowered. "—I'll… I'll say the words." She looked up quickly at the shadows on the wall and addressed them theatrically. "No! No! I mustn't. I mustn't. I mustn't say… 'I wish… I wish…'"

"Listen," said the goblin again.

Every glowing eye in the nest, every ear, was open now.

A second goblin spoke. "She's going to say it!"

"Say what?" asked a stupid goblin.

"Shush!" The first goblin was straining to hear Sarah.

"You shut up!" said the stupid goblin.

In the hubbub, the first goblin thought he would go crazy with trying to hear. "Sh! Shhh!" He put his hand over the mouth of the stupid goblin.

The second goblin shrieked, "QUIET!" and thumped those nearest to him.

"Listen," the first goblin admonished the rest. "She is going to say the words."

The rest of them managed to silence themselves. They listened intently to Sarah.

She was standing erect. Toby had reached such a crescendo of screaming, red in the face, that he could scarcely draw breath. His body was straining against Sarah's arms with the effort he was making. Launcelot had fallen to the floor again. Sarah closed her eyes and quivered. "I can bear it no longer," she exclaimed, and held the howling baby above her head, like a sacrificial offering. She started to intone:

"Goblin King!
Goblin King!
Wherever you may be,
Come and take this child of mine
Far away from me!"

Lightning cracked. Thunder crashed.
The goblins dropped their heads, crestfallen.
"That's not right," the first goblin said, witheringly.
"Where did she learn that rubbish? the second scoffed. "It doesn't even start with 'I wish.'"
"Sh!" said a third goblin, seizing his chance to boss the others.

Sarah was still holding Toby above her head. Outraged by that, Toby was screaming even more loudly than before, which Sarah would not have thought possible. She brought him down and cuddled him, which had the effect of restoring him to his standard level of screaming.

Exhausted by now, Sarah told him, "Oh, Toby, stop it. You little monster. Why should I have to put up with this? You're not my responsibility. I ought to be free, to enjoy myself. *Stop it!* Oh, I wish… I wish…" Anything would be preferable to this cauldron of noise, anger, guilt, and weariness in which she found herself. With a little tired sob, she said, "I wish *I did* know what words to say to get the goblins to take you away."

"So where's the problem?" the first goblin said with an impatient sigh. Pedantically, he spelled it out. "'I wish the goblins would come and take you away, right now.' Hmm? That's not hard, is it?"

In the nursery, Sarah was saying, "I wish… I wish…"

The goblins were all alert again, biting their lips with the tension.

"Did she say it?" the stupid goblin asked brightly.

As one, the rest turned on him. "Shut," they said irritably, "up."

Toby's tornado had blown itself out. He was breathing deeply, with a whimper at the end of his breath. His eyes were closed. Sarah put him back in his crib, not too gently, and tucked him in.

She walked quietly to the door and was shutting it behind her when he uttered an eerie shriek and started to scream again. He was hoarse now, and louder in consequence.

Sarah froze, with her hand on the handle of the door. "Aah," she moaned helplessly. "I wish the goblins *would* come and take you away…." She paused.

The goblins were so still, you could have heard a snail blink.

"… right now," Sarah said.

In the goblins' nest, there was an exhalation of pleasure. "She said it!"

In a trice, all the goblins had vanished in different directions, save only the stupid goblin. He squatted there, a grin dawning on his face, until he realized that the rest had left him. "Hey," he said, "wait for me," and he tried to run in several directions at once. Then he, too, vanished.

Lightning flashed and thunder hammered the air. Toby gave out with a high-pitched screech, and Merlin barked as if all the burglars in the world were closing in.

CHAPTER II
WHAT'S SAID IS SAID

The storm raged on over Sarah's house. The clouds boiled. Rain lashed the leaves on the trees. Thunder was followed by lightning.

Sarah was listening. What she was listening to was an unnatural silence within the room. Toby had stopped crying, so suddenly it scared her. She looked back inside the nursery. The bedside light was out. "Toby?" she called. He did not respond.

She flicked the light switch beside the door. Nothing happened. She jiggled it up and down several times, to no effect. A board creaked. "Toby? Are you all right? Why aren't you crying?"

She stepped nervously into the quiet room. The light from the landing, coming though the doorway, threw unfamiliar shadows onto the walls and across the carpet. In the lull between two thunderclaps, she thought she heard a humming in the air. She could detect no movement at all in the crib.

"Toby," she whispered in anxiety, and walked toward the crib with her breath drawn. Her hands were shaking like aspen leaves. She reached out to pull the sheet back.

She recoiled. The sheet was convulsing. Weird shapes were thrusting and bulging beneath it. She thought she glimpsed things poking out from the edge of the sheet, things that were no part of Toby. She felt her heart thumping, and she put her hand over her mouth, to stop herself from screaming.

Then the sheet was still again. It sank slowly down over the mattress. Nothing moved.

She could not turn and run away and leave him. She had to know. Whatever the horror of it, she had to know. Impulsively, she reached out her hand and pulled the sheet back.

The crib was empty.

For a moment or an hour, she would never know how long, she stared at the empty crib. She was not even frightened. Her mind had been wiped clean.

And then she was frightened, by a soft, rapid thumping on the windowpane. Her hands clenched so tightly, her fingernails scored her skin.

A white owl was flapping insistently on the glass. She could see the light from the landing reflected in its great, round, dark eyes, watching her. The whiteness of its plumage was illuminated by a series of lightning flashes that seemed continuous. Behind her, a goblin briefly raised his head, and ducked down again. Another did likewise. She didn't see them. Her eyes were fixed on the owl's eyes.

Lightning crackled and flashed again, and this time it distracted her attention from the window by shining on the clock that stood on the mantelpiece. She saw that the hands were at thirteen o'clock. She was staring distractedly at the clock when she felt something nudge the back of her legs. She glanced down. The crib was moving across the carpet on scaly legs like a lizard's, with talons for toes, one leg at each corner of the crib. Sarah's lips parted, but she made no sound.

Behind her, something snickered. She spun around and saw it duck down again behind the chest of drawers. Shadows were scuttling across the walls. Goblins were prancing and bobbing behind her. Sarah was watching the chest of drawers. Like the crib, it had a scaly, clawed foot at each corner, and it was dancing.

She wheeled around, mouth open, hands clenched, and saw the goblins cavorting. They ducked away into the shadows, to evade her eyes. She looked for something that would serve as a weapon. In the corner of the nursery was an old broom. She took it and advanced upon the goblins. "Go away. Go away," she whimpered, trying to sweep them up, but the handle of the broom twisted in her hands and slithered out of her grasp.

The storm wind rose to a pitch. Lightning made daylight in the room, and scared faces suddenly began to vanish into cupboards, drawers, or down the cracks between floorboards. As the thunder boomed and the wind shook the curtains, a blast of air blew the window open. Between the fluttering curtains the white owl entered.

Sarah wrapped her arms around her face, and screamed, and screamed again. She was petrified that the flapping owl would brush across her. She thought she would die if it did.

She felt the wind blowing her hair around, but the flapping had ceased. Between her fingers she peeked out, to see where the bird was perched. Perhaps it had flown out again.

A prolonged crackling of lightning was throwing a giant shadow on the wall facing the window. It was the shadow of a human figure.

Sarah spun around. Silhouetted against the stormy sky was a man. He wore a cloak, which swirled in the wind. She could see that his hair was shoulder-length and blond. Something glinted about his neck.

More than that she could not see in the dim light.

She said, "Uh...," and cleared her throat. "Who are you?"

"Don't you know?" The man's voice was calm, almost kindly.

Lightning traced the veins of the sky and lit up his face. He was not smiling, as one might smile on greeting a stranger, nor was his expression fierce. His eyes were fixed upon Sarah's with an intensity she found compelling. When he took a step toward her, into the light shining from the doorway, she did not retreat. If his eyes had not hypnotized her, the golden chain around his neck might have. A sickle-shaped ornament hung from it, upon his chest. His shirt was cream-colored, open at the front, loose-sleeved, with silken cuffs at the wrist. Over it he wore a tight, black waistcoat. He was shod in black boots, over gray tights, and on his hands were black gloves. In one of them he held the jeweled knob of a curious cane with a fishtail shape at the end.

"I...," Sarah answered. "I..."

The humming that she had thought she heard in the air was now quite distinct, and musical. The stranger smiled at her hesitancy. He was certainly handsome. She had not expected that. When she spoke, her voice was a whisper.

"You're... him, aren't you? You're the King of the Goblins."

He bowed. "Jareth."

She resisted the ridiculous impulse to return a curtsy.

"I have saved you," he said. "I have liberated you from those bonds that distressed you and frightened you. You're free now, Sarah."

"Oh, no. I don't want to be free," she answered. "I mean, I do, but—I want my little brother back. Please." She gave him a tiny smile. "If it's all the same to you."

Jareth folded his hands on the top of his cane. "What's said is said."

"But I didn't mean it," Sarah replied quickly.

"Didn't you, now?"

"Oh, please. Where is he?"

Jareth chuckled. "You know very well where he is."

"Please bring him back, please." She heard herself speaking in a small voice. "Please!"

"Sarah…" Jareth frowned, and shook his head. His expression was all concern for her. "Go back to your room. Read your books. Put on your costumes. That is your real life. Forget about the baby."

"No, I can't."

For a moment, they regarded each other, adversaries trying to size each other up at the outset of a long contest. Thunder rumbled.

Then Jareth raised his left arm, and made a large gesture with his hand. Sarah looked around, thinking that he was summoning assistance. When she faced him again, a glowing crystal had appeared in his hand.

"I've brought you a gift, Sarah," he said, holding it out to her.

She paused. She could not trust him. "What is it?"

"A crystal, nothing more. Except that if you look into it… it will show you your dreams."

Sarah's lips parted involuntarily. With a teasing smile, Jareth watched her face, while he spun the shining crystal around in his fingers. Her hand started to reach out for it. He smiled a little more, and withdrew the crystal from her.

Raising the cane with his other hand, he told her, "But this is not a gift for an ordinary girl, one who takes care of a screaming baby." His voice was quieter now, and huskier. "Do you want it, Sarah?" He held it out toward her again.

This time her hands remained by her sides, and she made no answer. Her eyes were fixed on the dancing, flashing glints of the crystal. To see her own dreams—what wouldn't she give for that?

"Then forget the child," Jareth said firmly.

While Sarah hesitated, another bolt of thunder and lightning illuminated the sky behind the Goblin King.

She was torn. The gift was not only seductive, it was also the choice of someone who understood her, someone who cared about the secret places of her imagination and knew how infinitely much more they meant to her than anything else. In return, she would have to trade her responsibility for an offensively spoiled child, who made endless demands upon her and never showed the least sign of gratitude; who was, after all, only her half brother. The crystal was spinning, glowing.

She willed her eyes to close. From behind shut eyelids, she heard a voice answering. It was her own voice, but it seemed to be a memory. "I—I can't. It isn't that I don't appreciate what you're trying to do for me... but I want my baby brother back. He must be so scared..." She opened her eyes again.

Jareth snorted, and tossed his mane of blond hair. He had lost patience with the girl. With a wave of his hand, he extinguished the crystal. With another wave, he plucked a live snake from the air. He held it with a straight arm in front of him, so that it writhed and hissed near Sarah's face. Then he threw it at her. "Don't defy me," he warned her.

It was wrapped around her neck. She clutched desperately at the thing, and found that it was now a silk scarf. She pulled it off, looked at it, and the snake came leaping out of the scarf. She yelled, dropped it and jumped away. When it hit the floor it shattered into a number of horribly ugly little goblins, who scuttled, snickering, to the corners of the room. Other goblins crept from the shadows, or popped out from their hiding places, and stood, all around the room, brazen now, watching to see what their king would do to her next.

"You are no match for me, Sarah." Jareth sounded impatient. "Let the child alone. Take my gift. I will not offer it to you again."

Before he could produce the crystal, Sarah told him, "No." She paused. "Thank you all the same, but I can't do what you want. Can't you see that? I must have my brother back."

"You will never find him."

"Ah," Sarah said, and took a deep breath. "Then… there *is* a place to look."

Just for a moment, Jareth's face flinched. Sarah saw it, the merest trace of fear fleeting across his eyes. Was it possible? His nostrils tightened, he gripped his cane, and appeared to hesitate slightly before answering her. She could not quite believe it, but the suspicion that the Goblin King could be afraid of her, even if only momentarily, was encouraging.

"Yes," he said. "There is a place."

And now, with a really hammy gesture straight out of vaudeville, he twirled his hand and pointed through the window.

"There!"

Lightning and thunder, right on cue, she thought. She moved past him and stared into the night. On a distant hill, brilliant in the flashes, she saw a castle. She leaned on the windowsill, trying to see more clearly. There were towers with turrets, massive walls, spires and domes, a portcullis and drawbridge. The whole edifice was built on top of a sharply rising mound. Around it the lightning flickered and forked like snakes' tongues. Beyond was blackness.

From just behind her shoulder, Jareth murmured, "Do you still want to look for him?"

"Yes." She swallowed. "Is that…" She remembered the words. "… the castle beyond the Goblin City?"

Jareth did not answer at once, and she turned around. He was still there, watching her intensely, but they were no longer in the house. They stood facing each other on a windswept hilltop. Between them and the hill on which the castle stood was a broad valley. In the darkness she could not tell what was down there.

She turned again. The wind blew her hair over her face. Brushing it back, she took one timid step forward.

Jareth's voice came from behind her. "Turn back, Sarah. Turn back, before it is too late."

"I can't. Oh, I can't. Don't you understand that?" She shook her head slowly, gazing at the distant castle, and to herself, quietly, repeated, "I can't."

"What a pity." Jareth's voice was low, and gentle, as though he really meant it.

She was looking at the castle. It seemed to be a long way off, but not impossibly far to travel. It depended on what she would encounter in the valley, how easily it could be crossed. Was the darkness down there perpetual? "It doesn't look that far," she said, and heard in her voice the effort she was making to sound brave.

Jareth was at her elbow now. He looked at her, with a smile that was icy. "It's farther than you think." Pointing at a tree, he added, "And the time is shorter."

Sarah saw that an antique wooden clock had appeared in the tree, as though growing from a branch. On it were marked the hours to thirteen, as on the nursery clock in the lightning.

"You have thirteen hours to unriddle the Labyrinth," Jareth told her, "before your baby brother becomes one of us."

"Us?"

Jareth nodded. "Forever."

Magic still hummed in the air. Sarah was standing still, hair tossing in the wind, looking out across the valley toward the castle. After a while, she said, "Tell me where I start."

She waited for an answer, and finally she heard him say, "A pity."

"What?" She turned her head to look up at him, but he was not there. She spun all around. He had vanished. She was alone in the night, on a windswept hilltop.

She looked across again at the castle. The storm was passing away. Blades of clouds sliced across the moon. She thought she glimpsed the figure of an owl, high above, wings spread wide on the air, as he flew steadily away from her.

She took another step forward, down the hillside. But there was no ground beneath her feet. She began to fall.

CHAPTER III
PIPSQUEAK

Sarah felt herself toppling forward, into the darkness. Only by swinging her arms wildly did she manage to keep her balance. The hillside was very steep.

Her mouth had gone dry with fright. Carefully, she sat down. That felt safer, but she could not afford to sit there long, with only thirteen hours to get through the Labyrinth and find Toby in the castle.

She tried slithering down the hillside on her bottom, but that was no good either. Rocks and little shrubs impeded her, and she dared not stand up to get past them. It was so black, she might have been trying to find her way through a sea of ink. She felt tears rising, but blinked them away. She would do it. There were no limits to what she could do, given the determination (which she certainly had), and the ingenuity (which she had never lacked yet, admittedly in more humdrum predicaments), and maybe a little luck (which she deserved, didn't she?). She would do it, she vowed, as she sat on the black hillside with no idea how to move another foot.

High above her, where the owl had flown, she heard a lark sing.

She peered up at it, and by taking her eyes off the blackness below she became aware that a hint of light was staining the rim of the dark sky. She watched the light grow brighter, changing from red to pink, and then pale blue, and when she saw the edge of the sun inch up over the horizon she shut her eyes and took a deep breath. She felt the sun warming her skin. She would do it.

When she opened her eyes again, Jareth's castle was shining before her, its spires and turrets rimmed with the reflected sunlight. Anxiously she scrutinized the valley, which, like a developing photograph, took longer to reveal itself.

The first thing she could gauge was its width. The extent of land between herself and the castle was not so very great. I can run that far in a couple of hours, she reckoned. It's only a few miles. Jareth was trying to hoax me. He thought I would be so scared in the darkness that I would give up and forget about Toby. How could I? Anyway, in thirteen hours I can be there and back with time to spare.

She wondered if thirteen hours in Jareth's land would take the same time to pass as at home. If so, what would her father and stepmother think when they returned? They would probably call the police. Well, there was nothing she could do about that. She did not expect to find a telephone in Jareth's castle. She smiled wanly.

The sun was above the horizon, and color and shape were seeping into the valley. There was an awful lot of stuff down there; she could tell that much. She went on watching, and gradually she took in the full nature of the valley.

At first she could not believe it. As the sun rose higher and disclosed more to her, her shoulders drooped and her face lost its smile. She shook her head slowly, dumbfounded.

From the foot of the hillside where she sat, to the castle and beyond it, and from horizon to horizon on each side, there stretched a vast, intricate maze of walls and hedges.

"The Labyrinth," she whispered. "So that is the Labyrinth."

She studied it, trying to decipher some pattern to it, some principle of design that might guide her through it. She could see none. Corridors doubled, and wound and coiled. Gateways led to gateways leading into gateways. It reminded her of thousands of fingerprints laid side by side, overlapping each other. Did someone work all that out, she wondered, or had it just happened?

The impossibility of ever finding her way through the Labyrinth started to overwhelm her. She stood up, clenched her fists, set her jaw, and cleared her throat. "Well," she said, "here we go. Come on, feet."

In the dawning light, she could see below her a path that zigzagged down the hillside. She picked her way to it through the rocks and shrubs. At the foot of the path, she came to a great wall, strengthened with buttresses. It stretched as far as she could see to the left and right.

Doubtfully, she approached the wall, with no idea what she might do when she reached it. As she got closer, a movement just at the base of it caught her eye. There was a little man. He was cackling as he ground something underfoot.

"Excuse me," Sarah said.

The little man nearly jumped out of his skin. "Just going," he said, before he had even looked around to see who it was.

When he did turn, he had his face down so that he regarded her from under his thick, bushy eyebrows. "Well!" he exclaimed, looking cross and astonished at the same time. "Well!" It seemed that he had never before set eyes on a person like Sarah. Or perhaps it was that no person like Sarah had ever caught him unawares. "Well!" he said again.

We'll never get anywhere like this, Sarah thought.

He was an odd little person. His sprouting eyebrows clearly wanted to be fierce, but his wrinkled face couldn't live up to that ferocity. His expression was wary now, not particularly friendly, but not hostile either. He seemed to be avoiding her eyes, and she noticed that whenever she moved her hands his gaze would follow them. On top of his head he wore a skullcap. From the belt that held his breeches up, he had a chain of ornaments dangling, costume jewelry as far as she could tell. She saw his mouth moving to say "Well!" again and interrupted quickly.

"Excuse me, but I have to go through the Labyrinth. Can you show me the way in?"

His mouth frozen in the formation of a W, he blinked at her once or twice. Then his eyes darted to one side. He rushed a few steps toward a bluebell, at the same time pulling a spray can from under his jacket. As he aimed the spray, Sarah saw that a diaphanous little fairy was emerging from the bluebell.

He sprayed it, with a couple of quick bursts. The fairy at once wilted, like a shriveling petal.

"Fifty-seven," he said with some satisfaction.

Sarah was shocked. "Oh, how *could* you?"

He answered with a grunt.

She ran to where the fairy was lying on the ground, wings quivering and shriveling. "Poor thing!" she exclaimed. She picked it up gently in her fingertips and turned accusingly to the fairy-slayer. "You monster."

She felt a sharp pain, as from broken glass. The fairy had bitten her finger.

"Oh!" Sarah dropped the fairy and stuck her finger in her mouth. "It *bit* me," she muttered around her finger.

" 'Course she did," the little man chuckled. "What do you expect fairies to do?"

"I…" Sarah was frowning, perplexed. "I thought they did—well, nice things. Like granting wishes."

"Ha!" His eyebrows went up, and he chortled. "Shows what you know then, don't it?" He raised his spray can and casually hit another bluebell with it. A second shimmering fairy fell down, turning brown like a leaf in autumn. "Fifty-eight," he said, and shook his head. "They breed as fast as I spray."

Sarah was still wincing as she sucked her finger. "Ooh," she complained. "It hurts." She took her finger from her mouth and shook it.

He walked to a plant nearly as tall as he was, tore off one of its broad, grayish leaves, and handed it to her. "Here," he told her. "Rub that on it."

She gratefully did what he told her. No sooner had she started rubbing than she dropped the leaf, clasped her finger with the other hand and hopped around in pain. "Ow!" she shouted. "That makes it worse. Much worse. OWWW!"

He was holding his sides with his pudgy little hands and roaring with laughter. " 'Course it do. Fancy rubbing one of *them* on a fairy bite. You don't know nothing, do you?"

Her face screwed up with pain, Sarah answered indignantly, "I thought you were giving it to me to make it better. Oh! Ooh!"

"You thought that too, did you? You've got a lot of opinions." He chuckled. "All of them wrong. And you've got grass all over the seat of your trousers!"

In spite of the pain in her finger, she had to glance over her shoulder, and she saw that he was right. It was from sliding down that hillside. Brushing off what she could, she realized that he was paying her back for having caught him unawares. "You're horrible," she told him.

"No, I'm not." He sounded surprised. "I'm Hoggle. Who are you?"

"Sarah."

He nodded. "That's what I thought." Spotting another fairy, he squirted her. To make sure, he stepped on this one and ground his foot around. The fairy squealed. "Fifty-nine," Hoggle said.

Sarah was thinking, still sucking her finger. He seemed to know about her. So he must have something to do with Jareth, mustn't he? Some kind of spy, maybe? Well, maybe. Yet he was not her idea of a spy. Spies weren't grumpy. They didn't play mean tricks on you. Did they? If all her opinions were wrong, as he'd said, then this one might be wrong, too. But in that case, she thought, supposing he is a spy, then it might be his job to persuade me that all my opinions are wrong when really they are all correct. And if they are all correct, he is not a spy. But that would mean he had no motive for persuading me that I'm wrong about everything, and so probably I am wrong about this, too, and so... supposing he is a spy... "Oh!" she exclaimed, in exasperation. It was like one of those drawings she had seen in a book at home, where the water seems to be flowing uphill, and yet you can never put your finger on just where the drawing is telling you a lie.

Hoggle tore a leaf from a different plant and offered it to her, with a sort of twinkling scowl on his face.

She took her finger from her mouth. The pain was easing now. She shook her head, and had to smile a little at that funny, wizened face of his.

His expression, in answer, went dark again. He looked at her mistrustfully. He was not used to being smiled at.

Well, she thought, there's nothing else to do. Whether or not he is here to spy on me, he is the only person I can ask for help. So she tried. "Do you know where the door to the Labyrinth is?"

He screwed up his face. "Maybe."

"All right, where is it?"

Instead of replying, he dodged to one side, raising his spray can. "Sixty."

"I said, where is it?"

"Where is what?"

"The door."

"What door?"

"The door into the Labyrinth."

"The door! Into the Labyrinth! Oh, that's a good one." He laughed, not kindly.

Sarah wanted to punch him. "It's hopeless asking you anything."

"Not if you asks the right questions." He was giving her a sidelong look. "You're as green as a cucumber."

"Well, what *are* the right questions?"

Hoggle stroked the top of his nose. "It depends on what you want to know."

"That's easy. How do I get into the Labyrinth?"

Hoggle sniffed, and his eyes twinkled. "Ah! Now *that's* more like it."

She thought she heard that music in the air again, the magic music that had hummed around the Goblin King.

"You gets in there." He nodded, indicating behind her. "You got to ask the right questions if you want to get anywhere in the Labyrinth."

Sarah had spun around. Now, in the great wall, she saw a huge, grotesquely designed gate. She stared at it almost accusingly. She could have sworn it had not been there before.

"There ain't no *door*, see?" Hoggle was explaining. "All you got to do now is find the key."

She looked back at him and then all around her. She saw at once that it was going to be no problem to find the key. Near her was a very small mat, and from each end of it an enormous key was sticking out.

"Well," she said, "that's simple enough."

She went over to the key and tried to pick it up. She could just manage to get one end of it off the ground, or the other, but the whole key was too heavy for her to lift up to the keyhole in the gate. She glared at Hoggle.

"I supposed it's too much to expect you to give me a hand?"

"Yes," Hoggle said.

She tried again, straining to lift it. It was hopeless. "Oh," she said. "This is so *stupid*."

"You mean *you're* so stupid," Hoggle corrected her.

"Shut up, you rotten little pipsqueak."

"Don't call me that!" Hoggle was agitated. "I am not a pipsqueak."

"Yes, you are," Sarah said. She was uneasily reminded of herself at a much younger age, at school, chanting cruel jibes at some tormented girl, but she persisted. "Yes, you *a-are*. Rotten little nasty ugly pipsqueak!"

Hoggle was beside himself with rage. "Don't call me that," he said hysterically. "*You!* Ha! You're so stupid you are, you take everything for granted."

"Pipsqueak! Pipsqueak!"

"I'm not. I'm not. Stop it! Stop it!"

"Nasty, creepy little pipsqueak!"

Hoggle collected himself and with some dignity told her, "If you weren't so brainless, you'd *try* the gate."

That stopped her short. She thought for a moment, then went to the gate and gave it a little push. It swung open.

"Nobody said it was locked," Hoggle observed.

"Very clever."

"You think *you're* so clever," Hoggle said. "You know why? Because you ain't learned nothing."

Sarah was peering cautiously inside the gate. She did not like what she saw. It was dark and forbidding in there. The music humming in the air seemed to be more intense. There was a smell of things rotting.

She gathered her courage and took two steps into the Labyrinth. Then she stopped short. A passageway ran across the entrance. It was so narrow, and the wall was so high, that the sky was a mere slit over her head. In the gloom, she heard a continual drip of water, echoing. She approached the farther wall, touched it, and pulled her hand away. It was dank and slimy, like mildew.

Hoggle's head was poking through the gateway behind her. "Cozy, ain't it?"

Sarah shuddered.

Hoggle's manner had altered. He was quiet, and it was almost possible to detect a hint of concern in his voice. "You really going to go in there, are you?"

Sarah hesitated. "I... yes," she said. "Yes, I am. Do you... is there any reason why I shouldn't?" She was clenching her fists. It did seem such a dreadfully gloomy place, inside the gate.

"There's every reason why you shouldn't," Hoggle replied. "Is there any reason why you should? Any really good reason?"

"Yes, there is." She paused. "So I suppose... I must."

"All right," Hoggle said, in a tone of voice that implied, on your own head be it. "Now," he asked, "which way will you go? Right or left?"

She looked one way and then the other. There was no reason to choose either one or the other. Both looked grim. The brick walls appeared to extend to infinity. She shrugged, wanting some help, but too proud to ask for it. "They both look the same," she said.

"Well," Hoggle told her, "you're not going to get very far, then, are you?"

"All right," she said crossly, "which way would you go?"

"Me?" He laughed without mirth. "I wouldn't go neither way."

"Some guide you are."

"I never said I was a guide, did I? Although you could certainly use one. You'll probably end up back where you started, given your record for being wrong."

"Well," Sarah snapped at him, "if that's all the help you're going to be, you might as well let me get on with it!"

"You know your problem?" Hoggle asked.

She took no notice, but tried to look determined to set out in one direction or the other. Left, right, she was thinking, that was the normal order. So in this abnormal place, she might as well try going to the right, mightn't she?

"I told you, you take too many things for granted," Hoggle went on. "This Labyrinth, for instance. Even if you get to the center, which is extremely doubtful, you'll never get out again."

"That's your opinion." Sarah moved to her right.

"Well, it's a better opinion than any of yours."

"Thanks for nothing, Hogwart."

"*Hoggle!*" His voice came echoing from the gateway, where he remained. "And don't say I didn't warn you."

Her jaw set, she strode out, between the damp and dire walls.

She had gone only a few strides when, with a mighty, reverberating *clang*, the gate closed behind her. She stopped, and could not resist returning, to see if the gate would open again. It wouldn't.

Hoggle was shut outside. The only sounds in the Labyrinth now were the drip of water, and Sarah's quick breathing.

CHAPTER IV
WHICH IS WHICH

Sarah took a deep breath and set off along the passageway again. A clump of lichen on the gatepost opened its eyes and watched her go. The eyes, on tendrils, had an anxious look, and when she had gone some distance away the clump, swiveling its eyes toward each other, commenced to gossip among itself. Most of it disapproved of the direction she had taken. You could tell that from the way the eyes looked meaningfully into each other. Lichen knows about directions.

When she had been walking for a while between the towering walls of the apparently endless passageway and gotten nowhere that looked different, she went on walking for a while more, and it was all the same. Another hundred steps, she told herself, and if I'm still getting nowhere I'll think of something else to do.

One, two... ninety-eight, ninety-nine. The walls stretched to eternity.

"Is this what a labyrinth is?" she said aloud, for the company of hearing her own voice. "There's not a single turn, or corner, or—anything. It just goes on, and on." She paused, thinking of what Hoggle had said to her. "But maybe it doesn't," she reasoned. "Maybe... I'm just taking it for granted that it does. Because that's all it's done so far, go on and on. It could do that forever—and I haven't got forever." She wished she knew how much of the thirteen hours remained to her. It wasn't fair, not knowing.

Taking another deep breath, she began to run. The only difference now was that the walls revealed their endlessness more quickly. She ran faster, skidding in mud, banging against the brick sides of the passage, faster and faster, and the walls stretched out ahead of her without turning or feature or end, until they began to spin above her head and she realized that she was collapsing, exhausted, tears running down her cheeks.

She lay in a heap, sobbing. A clump of lichen nearby stared down at her sympathetically, its eyes boggling.

When she had recovered, she opened her eyes very slowly, hoping she would see something different this time: a corner, a door, even her own bedroom. All there was to see were the two walls.

With a little yelp of frustration, she beat her fists upon one of the walls.

As though answering a doorbell, a tiny wormlike creature with large eyes popped its head out from between the bricks where Sarah had pounded. " 'Allo?" it asked in a cheery voice.

Woebegone, Sarah looked at the worm. A talking worm, she reflected; yes, I should never have taken it for granted that a worm can't talk. She shrugged. If a worm could talk, perhaps it could give her some advice. In a low voice, she asked it, "Do you know how to get through the Labyrinth?"

"Who *me?*" It grinned. "No, I'm just a worm."

Sarah nodded. She might have expected as much.

"Come inside and meet the missus," the worm invited her.

She managed a faint smile. "Thank you," she told the worm, "but I've got to get through the Labyrinth. And there are no turnings, or openings, or anything." She blinked away hot tears. "It just goes on and on."

"Ooh," the worm said, "you ain't looking right, you ain't. It's full of openings. It's just that you ain't seeing 'em, that's all."

Sarah gazed around in disbelief. The walls stretched away forever on either side.

There was no logic to it. Or maybe there was nothing but logic, and that was the trouble: all logic and no reason.

"There's an opening just across there," the worm went on. "It's right in front of you."

She looked. Brick wall, damp mildew, clump of lichen, nothing else. "No, there isn't."

The worm sniffed, and in a kind voice said, "Come in and have a nice cup of tea."

"There isn't an opening." Sarah's voice was insistent.

"You try walking that way, over there," the worm said, with a nod of encouragement. "You'll see. But first, why not have a nice cup of tea?"

"Where?" Sarah looked at the blank wall again.

"I got the kettle on."

The worm's hospitality was wasted on her. "That's just *wall*," she muttered. "There's no way through."

"Ooh," the worm observed, "this place, oh dear. Things aren't always what they seem, you know, not here. Not here, no. So don't you take anything for granted."

Sarah gave the worm a sharp glance. How was it that he had the same script as Hoggle? And in her mind she heard Hoggle's voice again. "Me? I wouldn't go neither way."

Neither way. Right in front of you. What else was there to do? She would try it. Very tentatively, flinching in anticipation, she walked into the wall, and through it, into another passageway.

Sarah was delighted. This passageway, too, stretched out infinitely to either side, but at least it was a different one. She turned back gratefully. "Thank you," she said to the worm. "That was incredibly helpful."

She had begun to walk along the new passageway when she heard a little shout from behind her. "And don't go that way!" the worm was calling. He looked up at the lichen, whose eyes were worried as they watched Sarah. The worm gave the lichen a cheerful grin, but the lichen just went on boggling anxiously after the girl.

She halted, and then came back panting. "What did you say?"

"What I said," the worm told her, "was, don't go that way."

"Oh," Sarah nodded. "Thanks." She set off in the other direction.

The lichen watched her go again, and sighed with relief.

"Whew." The worm rolled his eyes. "That was close. If she'd gone the other way, she'd have walked straight into that dreadful castle."

In the stone chamber of the Goblin King, Toby, still in his red-and-white-striped pajamas, had his mouth wide open and was howling. His little fists were clenched tight, his face was scarlet, his eyes were shut, and he was putting out a din that would have made Sarah groan aloud.

Jareth watched him with an amused smile. In that place no one else took much notice of Toby. Horned or hairy or helmeted goblins racketed around the place, across the filthy floor, over the steps of the throne, up on the ledges of the room, some chasing chickens or a black pig in a helmet, some squabbling over a tidbit, some peering into any vessel in the hope of finding something to eat, some just sitting and gnawing on bones, others staring balefully at all the rest through crazed eyes. The place was littered with half-finished platefuls of food, and rotting bits of meat and vegetable matter, garbage and junk. A small pterodactyl flapped around, taking its chances. The curved crown mounted heraldically above the throne, decorated with ram's horns, had been appropriated by a vulture for its nest. Or perhaps Jareth had installed the vulture there for his own amusement.

He needed something to keep him amused here. The goblins were, frankly, a bore. They were so stupid they couldn't find their own way through the Labyrinth. They were without wisdom or wit. In the old days, when many babies had been offered to him, Jareth had been more tolerant, reckoning that soon he would certainly find one who could be trained as a worthy companion to the throne, one whose young blood would serve to refresh Jareth's, whose high spirits would dispel the thoughts of aging that oppressed the King of the Goblins. As calls upon him to steal a child became rarer, so Jareth sank deeper into dejection. He avoided mirrors and reflecting water. He could feel that the corners of his mouth had tightened, and he needed no proof of the wrinkles that creased his brow when he did not deliberately narrow his eyes to tauten his skin.

Lounging in his draped throne, which was in the form of an interrupted circle, Jareth looked at the bawling figure of Toby. With any luck, he might grow up to be an intelligent goblin. He might make some jokes, or anyway see the point of Jareth's. He might be of some help in ruling this ramshackle empire. At the very least, he might have some fresh ideas about mischief. Two-headed sheep, curdled milk, banging pans, snatched nightclothes, barren fruit trees, shifted tables, moldy bread—Jareth had seen it all, much too often. But this lot, rooting and pratfalling around all day, still found such tired old clichés a perfect riot every time. Pitiful, they were.

Jareth yawned, and looked wearily around the room. The walls had been decorated with skulls and bats. Dear god, he thought. Skulls and bats yet. How jejune could you get? He looked hopefully at the clock. Half past three, the sword-shaped hands indicated. Another nine and a half hours to wait, until the goblin striker struck the thirteen. He would have to do something to pass the time.

He stood up from the throne, stretched his arms and paced restlessly. Another goblin came dashing past. Jareth reached down and picked him up by the scruff of the neck. The goblin's eyes boggled at his.

"You're a boggling goblin," Jareth said, with a forced laugh.

The rest of the goblins howled with merriment. Jareth had been their King for as long as they could remember, which was about four seconds at best, and they hoped he would be King forevermore.

Jareth winced with the pain of it all.

Sarah was wandering along brick corridors. They were still high and forbidding, but at least they didn't stretch out to the end of space and time, and sometimes there was a flight of steps, which made a nice change. Whenever she came to a fork or a turning and made a choice, she had found a sensible way of ensuring that she did not wander in circles: with the lipstick she had put in her pocket at home, she made an arrow on a brick at each junction, to show where she had come from. And whenever she put the lipstick away and walked off down her new corridor, a little creature would lift the marked brick, turn it upside down, and replace it, so that the arrow was not visible.

After she had marked eighteen arrows, a piece of the lipstick broke off as she was doing the next one. Determined to remain calm, she screwed another length out, and went on her chosen way, up some steps, into a chamber. Across the end of the passage behind her a squad of goblins rustled by, but Sarah's eyes were fixed on what lay ahead and she did not see them.

The chamber was a dead end. She peeked in every alcove and behind the buttresses, but there was definitely no way out. She shrugged, and retraced her steps to the nineteenth arrow. When she reached the corner, she looked for her arrow and could not see it. That's odd, she thought. I'm sure it was right here, at this corner, on that brick there. The bricks were blank. She frowned, and looked about her. On the floor she spotted the broken-off piece of lipstick. She looked again, hard, and still could see no arrow. That proved it, then. Something fishy was going on. She threw down the rest of the lipstick. "Someone's been rubbing out my marks," she said, loudly, certain that the culprit must be close enough to hear her. "What a horrid place this is! It's not fair!"

"That's right," a voice behind her said. "It's *not* fair!"

She jumped, and whipped around.

Behind her, in the chamber that had been a dead end, she now saw two carved doors in the wall, and a guard posted in front of each door. At least, she thought they must be guards, since they stood foursquare and were emblazoned with armor. But as she studied them she was not so sure. They were quite comic, really. Their enormous shields, which were curiously patterned with geometrical figures and scrolls and devices, looked extremely heavy, which would account for the straddle-legged stance each of them had. Poor things, she thought, they have to stand like that all the time just to stay upright. The one to her left had incredibly shifty eyes beneath his helmet, and she said to herself that she would call him Alf, after an uncle of hers with eyes like that; but then she reflected that his not-quite-identical twin to her right (she couldn't see his eyes at all because his helmet was too big for him) should therefore be called Ralph (R for Right, you see), and so mentally she corrected the spelling of the first one's name to Alph (not that it mattered to anyone, because she wouldn't be writing their names down).

Having settled, in her mind, the business of names, she noticed the most remarkable thing of all, which was that from underneath each shield peered another face, upside down, a little like a jack of spades gone wrong. The upside-down characters, whom she named Jim and Tim (the first rhymed pair that came to her mind), seemed to be hanging on to their uncomfortable positions by the great gnarled and horny hands she could see gripping the bottom of the shields. They must have added yet more to the burdens under which Alph and Ralph staggered.

It was Jim Upside Down who made her jump by addressing her. He added, "And that's only half of it."

"Half of what?" asked Sarah, twisting and ducking her head to get a good look at Jim's face. It would, she felt, have been faintly rude to remain upright. You had to adjust to people you met, even here.

"Half of twice as much," Jim replied.

"Twice as much as *what?*" Sarah was exasperated.

"Twice as much as half of it."

"Look." Sarah raised a finger and pointed to the back wall of the chamber. "This was a dead end a moment ago," she said.

"No." It was Tim Upside Down speaking now. "*That's* the dead end, behind you."

She stood upright again and turned around. He was right. The way by which she had come in here was indeed now barred by a solid wall. "Oh!" she exclaimed indignantly. "It's not fair. This place keeps changing. What am I supposed to do?"

"It depends who's doing the supposing," Jim said.

"Not half," Tim agreed.

"Try one of the doors," suggested Jim.

"One of them leads to the castle," Tim told her in a cheerful voice, "and the other one leads to certain death."

Sarah gasped. "Which is which?"

Jim shook his upside-down head. "We can't tell you."

"Why not?"

"We don't know!" Jim crowed triumphantly.

"But *they* do." Tim nodded confidentially at Alph and Ralph. That took some doing, upside down, Sarah thought.

"Then I'll ask them," she said.

Before she could say anything more, Ralph was speaking in a very slow, pedantic voice. "Ah! No, you can't ask *us*. You can ask only *one* of us." He appeared to have difficulty in getting the words out at all, especially the *C*'s and *K*'s.

"It's in the rules." Alph's voice came fast and sneering, and at the same time his eyes shifted uneasily. He was tapping a finger on some ciphers on his shield, which were presumably the rules. "And I think I should warn you that one of us *always* tells the truth, and one of us always lies. That's a rule, too." His glance flickered at Ralph. "*He* always lies."

"Don't listen to him," Ralph said, sententiously. "He's lying. I'm the one who tells the truth."

"That's a lie!" Alph retorted.

Jim and Tim were snickering behind their shields, rather insolently, she thought. "You see," Tim told Sarah, "even if you ask one of them, you won't know if the answer you get is true or false."

"Now wait a minute," she said. "I know this riddle. I've heard it before, but I've never figured it out."

She heard Ralph muttering to himself, "He's lying."

"*He's* lying," Alph replied.

Sarah was scratching her brow. "There's one question I can ask and it doesn't matter which one of them I ask it." She clicked her tongue, impatient with herself. "Oh, what *could* it be?"

"Come on, come on," Tim said tetchily. "We can't stand around here all day."

"What do you mean, we can't?" Jim snapped. "That's our job. We're gatekeepers."

"Oh, yes. I forgot."

"Be quiet," Sarah ordered. "I can't think."

"I tell the truth," Ralph declared pedantically, from under his helmet.

"Ooh!" Alph answered mechanically. "What a lie!"

Sarah was trying to work it out logically for herself. With a finger thoughtfully in the air, she reasoned, "The first thing to do is find out which one's the liar... but, no, there's no way of doing that. So... the next thing to do is to find a question you can put to either one... and get the same answer."

"Oh, that's a good one," Tim was guffawing. "One of us always tells the truth and the other one always lies, and you want to find a question we'll both give the same answer to? Oh, that'll be the day. That's a good one, that is. Oh."

Sarah narrowed her eyes. She thought she might have gotten it. "Now," she said, "whom shall I ask?"

Alph and Ralph pointed at each other.

With a little smile, Sarah said to Ralph, "Answer yes or no. Would *he*," and she pointed at Alph, "tell me that this door," she pointed at the door behind Ralph, "leads to the castle?"

Alph and Ralph looked at her, then at each other. They conferred in whispers.

Ralph looked up at her. "Uh... yes."

"Then the *other* door leads to the castle," Sarah concluded. "And this door leads to certain death."

"How do you know?" Ralph asked slowly. His voice was aggrieved. "He could be telling you the truth."

"Then you wouldn't be," Sarah replied. "So if you tell me he said yes, I know the answer was no." She was very pleased with herself.

Ralph and Alph looked dejected, feeling that they had obscurely been cheated. "But *I* could be telling the truth," Ralph objected.

"Then he would be lying," Sarah said, allowing herself a broad smile of pleasure. "So if you tell me that he said yes, the answer would still be no."

"Wait a minute," Ralph said. He frowned. "Is that right?"

"I don't know," replied Alph airily. "I wasn't listening."

"It's right," Sarah told them. "I figured it out. I never could until now." She beamed. "I may be getting smarter."

She walked to the door behind Alph.

"Very clever, I'm sure," Jim remarked disappointedly, and stuck his tongue out at her.

She stuck hers out back at him as she pushed open the door. Over her shoulder, as she left them, she said, "This is a piece of cake."

She stepped through the doorway, and fell straight down a shaft.

Sarah screamed. The top of the shaft was a fast-dwindling disk of light.

CHAPTER V
BAD MEMORIES

As she screamed, dropping backward down the shaft, Sarah realized that her fall was being slightly impeded by things brushing against her. Large, thick leaves they might be, or some sort of tough fungus sprouting from the walls of this pit. Whatever they were, she tried to grab hold of one, to save herself from the terrible smash she expected every instant. She was falling too fast.

Then, by blind chance, her wrist landed smack in one of the things, which at once closed firmly. With a jolt that almost disjointed her, she found herself dangling by one arm. "Oh!" she gasped in relief, and felt herself heaving for breath.

She looked down the shaft, to see how close she had been to breaking every bone. All she could see was a long tunnel, lined with the things that had broken her fall. She looked up. The doorway through which she had entered the shaft was very high above her.

As her eyes adjusted to the gloomy light, she saw what it was that had caught hold of her: a hand. All around her, protruding from the sides of the shaft, hands were groping in the air, like reeds under water.

Her relief gave way to a sick feeling: she was in the grip of a hand with no arm or body attached to it, and she had no apparent means of ever releasing herself. Perhaps they were carnivorous hands, or like those spiders that simply dissolved you away over a long period of time. She looked nervously up and down the shaft again, this time to see if there were any skeletons dangling there, as in a jungle trap. She saw none.

And now she felt other hands reaching for her and finding her, taking hold of her by the legs and the body. There were hands on her thighs, her ankles, her neck. She shuddered, and shouted, "Stop that!" Knowing it was futile, she called, "Help! Help!" She writhed, trying to shake them all off, and with her free hand reached out for a hold, in a despairing attempt to climb away. All she could see to grasp hold of was yet another hand. Hesitantly she put hers in it, and it responded immediately, grasping her hand firmly. With the idea of perhaps climbing up the hands as though on a ladder, she tried to free her wrist from the first hand. It was no good. Now she was more tightly held than ever, stuck in a web of hands.

"Help!" she whimpered.

She felt a tap on her shoulder, and turned her head to see what it was. To her bewilderment, she saw that hands to one side of her contrived to form themselves into a face of sorts, with finger-and-thumb circles for eyes and two hands working together to fashion a mouth. And the mouth spoke to her.

"What do you mean, 'Help'?" it said. "We *are* helping. We're the Helping Hands."

"You're hurting," Sarah told them. It was not quite true. Fear, rather than pain, was what afflicted her.

Now there were several more faces of hands around her.

"Would you like us to let go?" one of them asked.

Sarah glanced down the shaft. "Uh… no."

"Well, then," one of the mouths said. "Come on. Which way?"

"Which way?" she asked, nonplussed.

"Up or down?"

"Oh…" She was more confused. "Er…" She looked back up the shaft toward the light, but that would be a kind of retreat. She looked down, into the unknown, unfathomable abyss.

"Come on! Come on!" an impatient voice urged her. "We haven't got all day."

Haven't you? Sarah thought to herself.

"It's a big decision for her," said a sympathetic voice.

"Which way do you want to go?" asked an insistent one.

Everyone in the Labyrinth was so peremptory. *I've* got good reason to be in a hurry, Sarah felt. I've only got thirteen hours to find my baby brother, and heaven knows how much time has already gone by. But why are all these people—if you can call them people—so bossy?

"Come on! Come on!"

"Well, er…" Sarah still hesitated. Up was chicken, and down was dreadful.

Many faces were watching her indecisiveness. Several of them were snickering, covering their mouths with another hand.

She took a deep breath. "Well, since that's the way I'm pointed… I'll go on down."

"She chose down?" She heard the snickerers behind their hands. "She chose—*down!*"

"Was that wrong?" Sarah inquired timidly.

"Too late now," said one of the hand faces, and with that they started to hand her down the shaft, not roughly. She heard them singing something like a shanty.

"Down, down, down, down,
Down, hand her down, boys.
We'll all go to town, boys.
Down, down, down, down,
Down, hand her down, boys,
Never a frown, boys,
Down, down, down, down."

And down she went, far down, until she found herself held momentarily above a manhole, while Helping Hands removed the cover of it. Then the lowest hands let go of her, dropping her neatly down the manhole, and the last she saw of the hands was their waving goodbye, helpfully.

As she landed on the stone floor of a dark, small cell, the cover was replaced on the manhole, with a clunk.

In pitch darkness, Sarah sat down. Her face was blank.

The picture of her silent face was clearly beamed to a crystal in the chamber of the Goblin King.

"She's in the oubliette," Jareth observed.

The goblins cackled wickedly, dancing and prancing around. Their jaws gaped with merriment, and they slapped their thighs.

"Shut up," Jareth told them.

They froze. Their heads twitched around to look at their King. A sly goblin inquired, "Wrong laugh?"

"She shouldn't have gotten as far as the oubliette." Jareth was still staring at the picture of Sarah's face in the crystal. He shook his head. "She should have given up by now."

"She'll never give up," said a keen goblin.

"Ha." Jareth laughed mirthlessly. "Won't she? She'll give up soon enough when she has to start all over."

It pleased him to think of his Labyrinth as a board game; if you got too close to the winning square, you might find a snake taking you back to the start. No one had, and very few had gotten as far as this disturbing girl, who was too old to be turned into a goblin. Jareth examined her face in his crystal. Too old to be a goblin, but too young to be kept by him, damn her innocent eyes. She had to be sent back to square one immediately, before she became a serious threat to Toby, and he knew the snake for the job. "Hoggle!" he called, spinning the crystal.

Hoggle's face appeared in it.

"She's in the oubliette," Jareth said. "Get her back to the outer walls."

Hoggle cocked his head, grimacing. "She's quite determined, your Majesty. It won't be an easy—"

"Do it." Jareth flipped the crystal into the air, where it vanished like a bubble.

He chuckled, imagining Sarah's face when she found herself beside Hoggle's pond again. Then he threw back his head and roared.

The goblins watched him uncertainly. Was it all right to laugh now?

"Well, go ahead," Jareth told them.

With the simple glee that is natural to evil-hearted folk, the goblins launched themselves into their full routine of cackles and snickers. The keen goblin directed them, like a conductor, bringing them up to a crescendo of malign mirth.

Sarah sat on the floor of the black cell wishing she had asked the Helping Hands to take her up the shaft, toward the light. What could she hope for in this place?

Four of her senses sharpened in the darkness; she detected a little scratching sound. "Who's there? Who's there with me?" Her body was tense with alarm.

"Me," a gruff voice replied.

There was another noise of scratching, followed by a glare of light as a match ignited, and in turn set a torch aflame. Hoggle was sitting there, on a rough bench, holding the torch up so that he and Sarah could see each other.

"Oh," she said, "I am glad to see you, Hoggle." She was so relieved she could have hugged him.

"Yes, well," Hoggle said brusquely, as though he were slightly embarrassed by the situation. "Well, nice to see you, too."

Sarah went to stand beside him, in the torchlight. "What are you doing here? How did you *get* here?"

Hoggle shrugged, and half turned away. "I knows you were going to get into trouble soon as I sees you. So I—I've come to give you a hand."

A helping hand, Sarah thought, and shivered. She had had enough of them. "You mean," she asked, "you're going to help me unriddle the Labyrinth?"

"Unriddle the Labyrinth?" Hoggle answered scornfully. "Don't you know where you are?"

She looked about her. In the circle of torchlight she saw stone walls, stone floor, stone ceiling. One rough wooden bench was the only luxury.

"Oh, she's looking around now, is she?" Hoggle's scorn had turned to sarcasm. "I suppose the little miss has noticed there ain't no doors— just the hole up there?"

Sarah peered as hard as she could into the shadows, and realized that he was right.

"This," Hoggle was saying, "is an oubliette. The Labyrinth's full of them."

She was stung by his knowing, mocking tone of voice. "Really?" she replied, matching his sarcasm. "Now, fancy that."

"Don't try to sound smart," he told her. "You don't know what an oubliette is."

"Do you?"

"Yes," Hoggle said, with a touch of pride. "It's a place you put people to forget about them."

She remembered her verbs in French class, and, pleased with herself, said, "Of course. It comes from the French verb *oublier*, to forget. But you already know that, naturally."

Hoggle raised his chin to scratch it, at the same time letting his eyes roll portentously around the cell.

What he had said began to sink in, and Sarah looked at the flickering stone walls and shuddered. To forget about them… Was that what Jareth was doing with her? Just forgetting about her? She began to feel indignant. It wasn't fair. He had challenged her to this contest. All the odds were stacked against her, but she had made a brave enough start—he couldn't, now, just dump her in here to rot. Could he?

Hoggle had taken the torch and waddled into one corner of the oubliette. He beckoned her to follow. She did, casting a great shadow across the walls. Lying in the corner was a skeleton, on its back, knees bent, head propped against the wall.

She put her hand to her mouth and was about to scream, then thought better of it. She would force herself to remain cool.

"You see?" Hoggle was squinting up at her. "This Labyrinth is a dangerous place. No place for a little girl."

She looked at him. Who was he calling little?

He nodded at the skeleton. "That's how you'll end up if you keep going. In an oubliette, like him. Lot of bad memories in the Labyrinth, I can tell you. What you got to do, little missy, is get out of here.

"But I must find my baby brother."

"Forget all that. Now it so happens," Hoggle said, scratching his cheek with a forefinger, "that I knows a shortcut out of the whole Labyrinth from here."

"No," she said at once. "I'm not giving up now. I've come too far. I've done too well."

He nodded, and in a smooth voice assured her, "You've been wonderful." He shook his head, and made a sucking noise on his teeth. "But this is only the edge of the Labyrinth. You've hardly started. From here on in, it gets worse."

There was something in his confidential tone that made Sarah suspicious. "Why are you so concerned about me?" she asked him.

"What?" Hoggle sounded aggrieved. "I *am*. That's all. Nice young girl... terrible black oubliette..."

"Listen," Sarah interrupted him, "you like jewelry, don't you?"

He pursed his face. "Why?" he asked slowly.

"You've got some very nice pieces." She pointed to the chain of ornaments dangling from his belt. In the torchlight she could not be sure, but she fancied that a smirking little blush was on his whiskery cheek.

"Thank you," he said.

"If you'll help me through the Labyrinth..." She took a breath. "...I'll give you..." She slipped her bracelet off. It was only a cheap plastic thing, not one of the special ones that her mother had given her, and which she wore when she was going out. "...*this*," she concluded, holding it out to him.

"Hm." Hoggle licked his lips and eyed the bracelet appraisingly.

"You like it, don't you?" She could see that he did. He also had an eye for the ring on her finger. That had no intrinsic value either, though Sarah was fond of it because her mother had worn it when playing Hermione in *The Winter's Tale*.

"So-so," Hoggle said. "Tell you what. You give me the bracelet and here's what I'll do. I'll show you the way out of the whole Labyrinth. How's that?"

"You were going to do that in any case," she pointed out.

"Yes," he replied. "That's what would make it a particularly nice gesture on your part." He held his hand out.

"Oh, no!" Sarah withdrew the bracelet abruptly. "For this you must show me the way *in*. The whole way."

Hoggle snorted. "What makes the little miss so certain *I* knows my way through it?"

"Well," she answered, "you got here, didn't you?"

"What?" Hoggle clucked, shaking his head. "Yes, yes, but... I told you, this is just the fringe of it all. You've got nowhere yet. Come on, where's your common sense? You don't want to go farther than this. Really. You've done all you can, and more. You have proved you're a smart, brave girl, and you don't deserve what would become of you in here." He glanced pointedly at the skeleton, which seemed to be jiggling in the flicker of the torchlight. "No, no, you deserve to be saved from that. I'll say that much for you. So—how about it?" He gazed up at her with eyes of piggy shrewdness from beneath his sprouting eyebrows.

She looked back at him candidly. Whatever his game was, he played it badly. She had to bite her lip to stop herself from giggling at him. "I'll tell you what," she said, narrowing her eyes. "If you won't take me all the way through the Labyrinth, just take me as far as you can. And then I'll try to do the rest of it myself."

He looked disgusted with her. "Tcha! Of all the headstrong numbskulls I ever came across…"

Sarah dangled the bracelet before his eyes. "Fair deal," she offered. "No strings. One bracelet. Hmm? How about it?"

The bracelet danced in her hand, and his eyes were dancing with it. Grudgingly he asked, "What is this, anyway?"

"Plastic."

His eyes shone. Then he raised his stumpy arm for Sarah to put the bracelet onto his wrist. He looked at it there and could not conceal his pride. "I don't promise nothing," he said. "But"—he grunted resignedly— "I'll take you as far as I can. Then you're on your own. Right?"

"Right," Sarah agreed.

He nodded. His eyes were still shining as he looked at the bracelet on his wrist. "Plastic!" he murmured, thrilled.

"Come on, then," Sarah urged him.

Hoggle sprang into action. He seized the heavy wooden bench and, with a strength Sarah wouldn't have suspected in his small and round-shouldered body, he upended it so that the seat was flat against the wall. Sarah was surprised to see two doorknobs on the underside of the seat, one on the left and one on the right, and she was disconcerted when Hoggle turned one knob and the seat became a door into the stone wall. That's not fair, she thought. With a mischievous grin—because he was enjoying himself, showing off to the young miss—Hoggle walked through the doorway.

She was about to follow him when she heard a crashing and clattering. Broomsticks and buckets fell out of the doorway into the oubliette. She grinned, recognizing the old broom-closet joke.

"Oh, damn!" she heard Hoggle say, within the cupboard. He came out backward, and avoided her eye as he thrust the brooms and buckets back inside and closed the door.

Still sheepish, he grasped the other doorknob. "Can't be right all the time, can we?" he muttered. This time, he opened the door rather less boldly. He peered through. "This is it," he told her. "Come on, then."

She followed him into a dimly lit corridor with walls of grotesquely carved rock.

They were working their way along the corridor when a voice boomed, "DON'T GO ON!"

Sarah jumped violently, and looked all around her. She saw no one, except Hoggle. And then she realized: carved in the stone wall was a mouth. Standing back from it, she saw that the mouth was part of a huge face. Similar faces lined both sides of the corridor. As she and Hoggle passed them, each intoned a deeply resonant message.

"Go back while you still can!"

"This is not the way!"

"Take heed and go no farther!"

"Beware! Beware!"

"It will soon be too late!"

Sarah put her hands over her ears. The warnings seemed to be echoing inside her head.

Hoggle, bustling onward, looked around to see where she had gone to, and saw her standing. "Pah." He waved his hand. "Don't take no notice of them. They're just Phony-Warnings. You get a lot like them in the Labyrinth. It means you're on the right track."

"Oh, no, you're not," a face boomed.

"Do shut up," Hoggle snapped back at it.

"Sorry, sorry," the face said. "Only doing my job."

"Well, you don't need to do it to us," Hoggle answered, and led the way on down the passage.

The face watched them go. "Shrewd cookies," it murmured appreciatively.

The passageway twisted and turned, but on the whole Sarah had the impression that they were moving forward, if such a direction existed in the Labyrinth, and she felt encouraged. They passed another carved face.

"Oh, beware!" the face declaimed. "For—"

"Don't bother." Hoggle flapped his hand dismissively.

"Oh, *please*," the face begged. "I haven't said it for such a long time. You've no idea what it's like, stuck here in this wall, and with—"

"All right," Hoggle told it. "But don't expect us to take any notice."

The face brightened up. "Oh, no, of course not." It cleared its throat. "For the path you take will lead you to certain destruction!" It paused. "Thanks," it added politely.

While the face was droning on, a small crystal ball had been rolling and skipping down the passage from behind Sarah and Hoggle. It overtook them as they turned a corner, and they saw it bounce on ahead of them. A blind beggar squatted with his back to the wall, his hat upturned on the ground in front of his feet. The crystal ball hopped smartly into the hat.

Sarah heard Hoggle groan. She looked at him. His mouth was open, and his eyes were staring at the hat on the ground.

The beggar turned his face toward them. "So what have we here?" he asked.

"Uh, nothing," Hoggle spluttered.

"Nothing? *Nothing?!*" The beggar rose up.

Hoggle froze. Sarah gasped. It was Jareth.

"Your Majesty…" Hoggle bowed so obsequiously that he was at

risk of performing a forward roll. "What…" he swallowed, and smiled haggardly, "what… what a nice surprise."

"Hello, Hedgewart," said the King of the Goblins.

"Hogwart," Sarah corrected him.

"*Hoggle*," Hoggle said, gritting his teeth.

"Hoggle," Jareth said, in a kindly conversational voice, "can it be that you're helping the girl?"

"Helping?" Hoggle prevaricated. "In what sense? Uh…"

"In the sense that you're taking her farther into the Labyrinth," Jareth said.

"Oh," Hoggle replied. "In *that* sense."

"Yes."

"Oh, no, no, your Majesty. I was leading her back to the beginning."

"What!" Sarah exclaimed.

Hoggle forced his lips into an ingratiating smile for Jareth. "I told *her* I was going to help her unriddle the Labyrinth—little trickery on my part…" He guffawed and gulped. "But *actually*…"

Jareth, smiling pleasantly, interrupted him. "And what's this plastic trinket around your wrist?"

"This? I…" Hoggle looked wide-eyed at the bracelet, which someone must have slipped onto his wrist when he was snoozing and which he had unaccountably not even noticed there until this moment. "Why," he stuttered, "er, my goodness, well, I never, where did this come from?"

"Hoggle." Jareth spoke levelly. "If I thought you were betraying me, I would be forced to suspend you *headfirst* in the Bog of Eternal Stench."

"Oh, no, your Majesty." Hoggle's knees were wobbling. "Not that. Not the Eternal Stench."

"Oh, *yes*, Hoggle." Jareth turned and smiled at Sarah. "And you,

Sarah—how are you enjoying the Labyrinth?"

Sarah swallowed. Beside her, she heard Hoggle's feet shuffling. Determined not to allow Jareth to intimidate her, she affected a nonchalance she was far from feeling.

"It's…" she hesitated. "It's a piece of cake."

Jareth raised one elegant eyebrow.

Hoggle's eyes closed in dismay.

"Really?" Jareth sounded intrigued. "Then how about making it a more entertaining challenge?"

He looked up, and in the space of air before his eyes the thirteen-hour clock appeared. He gestured gracefully, and the hands visibly began to turn faster.

"That's not fair," Sarah said.

"You say that so often. I wonder what your basis for comparison is."

Jareth took the crystal ball from his hat and tossed it back down the tunnel again. At once, from the darkness, came a noise: a crashing, whirring, trundling noise, distant as yet, but getting closer all the time, and louder.

Hoggle's face was a mask of panic. Sarah found herself instinctively shrinking away from the approaching din.

"The Labyrinth is a piece of cake, is it?" Jareth laughed. "Well, now we can see how you deal with this little slice." While his mocking laugh still rang, he vanished.

Sarah and Hoggle stared along the passageway. When they saw what was coming at them, their jaws dropped and they trembled.

A solid wall of furiously spinning knives and chopping cleavers was bearing inexorably down upon them. Dozens of keen blades glittered in the light, every one of them pointing forward and whirring wickedly. The wall of blades completely filled the tunnel, like a subway train, and it would chop them into little pieces in the blink of an eye. And, Sarah noticed with horror, along the bottom of the slashing machine was a busy row of brushes, for tidying up after itself.

"The Cleaners!" Hoggle shrieked, and took off.

"What?" Sarah was so terrified she was mesmerically rooted where she stood.

"Run!" Hoggle's shout came echoing back from some distance away and brought her to her senses. She dashed after him.

The slashing machine came clanking and trundling remorselessly on behind them.

All it needed for the story to finish now was that they should come to a dead end. Around a corner, they found one. A heavily barred door closed the tunnel in front of them.

CHAPTER VI
UP AND UP

Sarah gasped. The whizzing blades were rapidly drawing nearer.

Hoggle was pawing pathetically at the great door and mumbling to himself.

But Sarah wasn't listening to him. She was looking around for an escape—above, below. She dashed along the side walls, looking for a handle or button. There had to be some way out. That was how the Labyrinth worked. There was always some trick, if only she could find it.

The clanking, whirring, seething, brushing noise was louder. She glanced momentarily at what Hoggle was doing. He was still just scrabbling at the door. It was no use trusting to him. What could she do? What?

Her eye fell on a part of the wall, to one side of the door, that looked distinct from the rest, a panel of metal plates. She pushed at it and felt it give a little.

"Hoggle!" she shouted above the echoing din.

"Sarah!" he answered, hammering his pudgy fists against the door and kicking at it, as though it could be expected to relent in the face of such frustration. "Don't leave me!"

"Get over here and help me," she yelled back at him.

Hoggle joined her. Together they shoved with all their weight at the metal plates.

"Come on," Sarah told him, "*push*, you little double-crosser. *Push!*"

Hoggle was pushing. "I can explain," he panted.

"PUSH!"

The panel caved in suddenly. They fell through the space it left and sprawled flat on it.

Behind them, the machine slashed through the air just beside their feet. When it reached the great barred door, there was a terrible crunching sound as the knives and cleavers bit through the wood, spitting it out as splinters, which the whirling brushes swept up neatly. The machine was cranked along by four goblins, standing on a platform behind the wall of knives. They were grunting and sweating with the effort of turning handles and working levers to keep the contraption whirring. The racket clattered onward, through the demolished doorway, and off into the distance.

Sarah lay on her back, recovering her breath. Hoggle looked down at her. "He's throwing everything at us," he said, and shook his head with a trace of admiration. "The Cleaners, the Eternal Stench—the whole works. He must think a lot of you."

Sarah answered with a faint, forced smile. "He's got some funny ideas."

Hoggle was busy again. Eyes darting left and right beneath his bushy eyebrows, he clumped around in the shadows until he found what he was looking for. "This is what we need," he called. "Follow me."

She sat up and looked. There, on the floor of the tunnel they had entered, she saw the base of a ladder. It led up into darkness.

"Come on," Hoggle was calling. The first rung was too high for him to reach, and he was hopping around trying to jump up to it.

Sarah went over to him. The ladder looked unsafe to her. It was constructed of an odd assortment of bits of wood, planks, and branches, patched together with ends of rope and half-driven nails.

"Come on, give me a hand," Hoggle urged.

She stood with one hand holding the ladder. "How can I trust you," she asked, "now that I know you were taking me back to the start of the Labyrinth?"

"I *wasn't*," Hoggle protested, and stared fiercely at her with those piggy eyes of his. As a liar, he was so bad it was quite touching. "I told *him* I was taking you to the start of the Labyrinth, to throw him off the scent, d'you see? Heh-heh. But actually—"

"Hoggle." Sarah smiled reproachfully at him. "How can I believe anything you say?"

"Well," he replied, screwing up one eye, "let me put it this way. What choice do you have?"

Sarah thought about it. "There is that."

"And now," Hoggle said, "the main thing is to get back up." And he started again to try and hop up to the first rung of the rickety ladder.

Sarah gave him a leg up, watched him start, and followed. At any moment she thought the thing might collapse; but then, as Hoggle had said, what choice did she have?

Without turning his head, Hoggle called out, "The other main thing is not to look down."

"Right," she called back, and, as though it were a playground dare, she had to snatch a little look past her feet. "Ooooh!" she cried. They had climbed much higher than she would have thought possible in the time. The wobbly ladder seemed to stretch down below her forever. She could not see the bottom of it, nor could she see the top. She felt unable to climb another rung. Clutching the sides of the ladder, she started to shake. The whole ladder shook with her.

Above, Hoggle clung desperately to the shaking ladder. "I said *don't* look down," he moaned. "Or perhaps *don't* means *do* where you come from?"

"I'm sorry, I didn't realize…"

"Well, when you've done all the shaking you want, perhaps we could continue."

"I can't help it," Sarah wailed.

Jumping around like a monkey on a stick, Hoggle managed to answer, "Well, we'll just have to stay here until one of us falls off, or we turns into worm food."

"I *am* sorry," Sarah told him, still shaking.

"Oh, good. She's sorry. In that case, I don't mind being shaken off to my certain death."

Breathing deeply, and looking resolutely upward, Sarah forced herself to think of happy, secure things: Merlin, her room, lovely evenings out with her mother, multiplication tables. It worked. She gained control of her body and started to climb again.

Hoggle felt her coming, and he went on, too. "See," he called to her, "you've got to understand my position. I'm a coward, and Jareth scares me."

"What kind of position is that?"

"A very humble one. That's my point. And you wouldn't be so brave, either, if you'd ever smelled the Bog of Eternal Stench. It's… it's…" It was his turn to pause on the ladder, and control his shakes.

"What is it?"

"It makes me feel dizzy just to think of it."

"Is that all it does?" Sarah asked. "Smell?"

"Believe me, that's enough. Oh, dear me. You wait, you just wait, if you get that far."

"Can't you hold your nose?"

"No." Hoggle shuddered again, but started to climb. "Not with this smell. It gets into your ears. Up your mouth. Anywhere it can get in."

Sarah thought she could see the top at last. There were chinks of daylight above her head.

"But the worst thing," Hoggle continued, "is if you so much as get a splash of the mire on your skin you will never, *never* be able to wash the stench off."

He was on the top rung now. He reached up, fiddled with a sliding bolt and pushed open a wooden hatchway.

Outside was a clear blue sky. Sarah had never seen anything so beautiful.

CHAPTER VII
THE MEANING OF LIFE

Sarah joined Hoggle on the top rung of the ladder, gratefully clutching the side of the open hatchway. It felt like firm land after a voyage at sea.

They were looking at a garden, where birds were singing. It was surrounded by well-trimmed hedges—box hedges, she thought, and indeed they ran so straight, with neatly cut openings in them, and turned such precise right angles, and the lawn was so flat and tidy, that the garden was like a green box, with the blue sky for a lid. But that was not *why* they were called box hedges, was it? It was a rather formal garden, with carefully positioned stone monuments. On the stones were runic carvings, and a few faces—more of those Phony-Warnings, Sarah decided, preparing herself for gloomy predictions.

The hatchway through which they had emerged was itself the top of a large ornamental urn, set upon a marble table. What a ridiculous arrangement, Sarah reflected, as they clambered out of the urn and stepped down to the lawn. Nothing was what it seemed to be. It was like a language in which all the words were the same as your own, but where they meant something quite different from what you were used to. From now on, she would take nothing at its face value. She looked with suspicion at the urn, and then down at the grass. She stepped carefully. It could turn out to be the top of someone's head.

Hoggle spread his hands. "Here we are then. You're on your own from here."

"What?"

"This is as far as I goes."

"You…"

"Said I didn't promise nothing." He shrugged, callously.

"But you…"

"And you said you didn't need anyone to save you."

"You little cheat!" Sarah was outraged. "You nasty *little* cheat!"

"I'm not a cheat. I said I'd take you as far as I could go. Well, this is it."

"You're lying. You're a coward and a liar and—and—"

He sniffed. "Don't try to embarrass me. I have no pride."

"Pipsqueak!"

"Don't say that." Hoggle tightened his fists.

"Nasty double-crossing little runty cheating no-good pipsqueak!"

"I said, don't say that!" His eyebrows beetled.

She leaned toward him, and whispered, "Pipsqueak."

"*Arrgh.*" Hoggle's body clenched. He bared his teeth, then opened them to scream. With his feet together, he jumped in the air, thumping the ground as he landed. Then he lost his balance, and rolled on the grass, beating his fists in the air, kicking his stumpy legs. His voice alternated between a growl and a scream. "It was you insisted on going on. I said I'd get you out, but oh, no, you're so clever. You knew better, didn't you? *Arrgh.* Well, now you're on your own, and good luck to you, and good riddance." He closed his eyes, and rolled on the grass again.

Sarah watched him, her mouth open in amazement. She had never seen anyone so angry, not even Toby.

Eventually Hoggle subsided, and lay for a while, his eyes still closed, his body twitching occasionally. Sarah wondered if he needed some sort of help. She felt guilty. She had provoked all that with just her one word, which was clearly more hurtful than sticks or stones.

Hoggle opened his eyes. He did not look at her as he stood up, brushed himself down, and pretended he had enough dignity left to turn away with his head held high. "Hoggle won't be coming back to save you this time," he informed her.

"Oh, yes, he will," Sarah muttered under her breath. And before he could get away, she darted forward and snatched the chain of brooches and badges from his belt. She had to tug quite hard to get it off, and he staggered forward.

"Hey!" he protested.

"Ha-ha!" She held his precious jewelry too high for him to reach.

He danced around beneath the dangling chain, trying to jump up and grab it. It was no good. "Give that back!" he shrieked.

"No. You can have it back when I get to the center of the Labyrinth."

"But you heard Jareth," Hoggle whined. "The center is farther than I can go. No! No!" His whine had risen to a shrill whimper. "*Upside down in the Bog of Eternal Stench,*" he said. His eyes closed, and he shuddered.

"Now there's the castle," Sarah said, in a deliberately matter-of-fact voice, one a parent might use to a child after its tantrum. Over the hedges, she could see the castle's spires and turrets and towers gleaming in the sunlight, and she pointed to them. "Which way should we try?"

"I don't know." Hoggle had turned sullen.

"Liar."

"Give it back!" Hoggle was trying to leap up and grab the chain again. "Give it *back!*"

She ignored him. "Let's try this way," she proposed, and walked smartly through one of the gaps in the hedges, into a hedged alley.

Hoggle followed her reluctantly, his chin on his chest.

She led the way down the straight alley, and soon came out into another garden, very like the one they had just left. Indeed, it was so like the first garden that... it *was* the same one, she realized. She went to the urn, and lifted the lid, to check. Yes, there was the ladder leading downward. She frowned. "Isn't this the place we just came from?"

Hoggle was paying no attention to anything but his string of baubles. "You—you..." He leaped, but could get no more than half an inch off the ground. "Give it back!" he bellowed.

"I'm sure it's the same place." Sarah stared at the hedges and decided to try another gap. "Come on," she told Hoggle, "let's try down here."

He trotted miserably after her.

Again the alleyway ran geometrically straight, at a right angle to the hedge bordering the garden, and again, within a few strides, they emerged into a garden so very like...

Sarah groaned. "Oh, *no*." They had come out through a gap directly facing the one they had entered.

"Give me my things." Hoggle was trying on a tone of menace. It was easy to ignore.

"Come on," Sarah said, undaunted, and tried a different gap.

The result was the same as before. They were facing the gap they had entered, and Hoggle was watching nothing but his jewelry. Sarah scratched her head. "I don't believe it," she muttered, and looked around the garden. "Which one haven't we tried?"

Hoggle pointed at a gap.

"Well, let's try that one, then." She plunged into the gap.

This time, Hoggle didn't follow her, but waited, arms folded, on the lawn. It was only a moment before she reappeared.

"Oh," she groaned, "it's impossible."

"She's so clever, is she?" Hoggle sneered. "Thinks she can do it all. And she's lost before she's even started."

Sarah turned on him. "There's no point in sounding so smug. If you don't help me, you won't get your stuff back."

"But…" Hoggle's face fell. "I don't *know* which way to go," he admitted.

"Then you'll have to help in some other way, won't you?"

"Them is my rightful property," Hoggle complained. "It's—it's not *fair.*"

"No, it isn't," Sarah conceded. She found herself smiling, and it took her a moment to realize why. Then she saw it, like a conundrum that would never fool her again. Nothing was fair. If you expected fairness, you would be forever disappointed. She turned a broad grin upon Hoggle. "That's the way it is."

At that moment, she spotted a curious robed figure strolling across the lawn, apparently deep in thought. Where had he come from? He was an old man, with a long white mustache and white eyebrows, but the most striking thing about him was his hat, which was topped with the head of a bird, with a sharp beak and eyes that were darting glances everywhere.

"Excuse me," Sarah called, running across the lawn after the old man. With his slow stride, furrowed brow, bent head, and hands clasped behind his back, he appeared very wise. Surely he could be of more help to her than the runty pipsqueak she had had to rely upon till now. He was settling gravely down on a garden bench as she approached. "Please," she said, "can you help me?"

The Wise Man didn't really register Sarah's presence. It was true that he raised his face toward her, but only as one might gaze at a tree, a fly, or a cloud while lost in thought. Rather than her, he seemed to be seeing a far horizon beyond her, so far beyond that few mortals had ever scanned it.

The depth and range of his thinking was clearly vast, whatever the subject of his thoughts might be. He was probably pondering deeply upon some problem that Sarah had never even imagined. Was it mathematical, she wondered, like the square root of negative two? Or philosophical, the meaning of meaning, perhaps? But no, those were things she'd at least tried to imagine, when she had read about them. Those great eyes gazing right through her were more likely preoccupied with some question of physics, or biochemistry, or linguistics, or all of that at once and more.

"Please?" she repeated timidly.

The bird's head on the Wise Man's hat suddenly spoke. "Go away! Can't you see he's thinking?"

The Wise Man slowly raised a finger, and rolled his eyes up toward the bird, and spoke. "Sh," he said.

Sarah closed her mouth apologetically. She stood aside, and waited.

"And don't stare," the hat reprimanded her. "You'll put him off."

"I'm sorry."

The Wise Man's lips opened slowly, and his eyes turned upward again, to address the hat. "Silence," he commanded.

The hat looked wryly at Sarah. "This is the thanks I get," it said disgustedly.

"Where was I?" the Wise Man was asking.

"How should I know?" the hat chirped. "You're the Big Thinker."

The Wise Man noticed Sarah. "Ah, a young girl."

Sarah returned a polite little smile.

The Wise Man's gaze traveled downward, and settled on Hoggle. "And is this your brother?"

"Oh, no," Sarah answered. "He's just a friend."

Hoggle had been about to expostulate at being taken for Sarah's brother, but now he stopped, and looked sideways at Sarah. It was the first time anyone had called him a friend. He frowned.

The Wise Man took a long breath. "And what can I do for you?" he asked Sarah.

"Please," she said, feeling shy and a little confused to be conversing with an ancient sage about what must seem to him so trivial a matter, "can you tell me... we—er, that is, *I* must get to the castle... But I can't even get out of this garden. Every time I try to leave I find myself right back here again. I can see the castle over there, but... can you tell me, please, how I can get to it?"

"Ah." The Wise Man nodded slowly, closing his eyes. After a while he said, "So you want to get to the castle."

"How's *that* for brain power?" demanded the bright-eyed hat.

"Quiet," the Wise Man commanded.

"Nuts," the hat replied.

Sarah put a hand over her mouth to conceal a giggle.

The Wise Man composed his hands together on his lap. "So, young woman," he told her, pursing his lips in thought. Nodding, he explained, "The way forward is sometimes the way back."

His hat pulled a face. "Will you listen to this crap?"

The Wise Man was glaring upward and clenching his fingers. He cleared his throat. "And sometimes," he continued, gazing earnestly at Sarah again, "the way backward—"

"Is the way forward," the hat interrupted. "Can you believe it? I ask you."

"Will you be quiet!" the Wise Man ordered his hat, profoundly. He looked again at Sarah. "Quite often, young lady, it seems we're not getting anywhere, when in fact we are."

Sarah looked despairingly around the garden. "Well, I'm certainly not getting anywhere at the moment."

"Join the club," said the hat.

"Perhaps," the Wise Man said, "perhaps it only seems like that. All… is not always… what…" It appeared that he was drifting off into a reverie, on the nature of good and evil, possibly, or four-dimensional calculus, and he only just made it to the end of his sentence, "…it seems."

The hat peered down over the Wise Man's forehead, then looked perkily up at Sarah and Hoggle. "I think that's your lot," the hat said. "The sum total of earthly wisdom strewn at your feet for the asking. Please leave a contribution in the box."

Sarah noticed for the first time that the Wise Man had absentmindedly drawn a collection box, with a slot, from the folds of his robe, and now was sitting, quite abstracted in contemplation, with the box on his knee. As she looked at it, he gave it a discreet little shake.

What was she to do? She hesitated, then had the idea of donating one of the badges from Hoggle's string, which she was still holding.

He read her mind. "Don't you dare!" Hoggle barked. "Them's mine."

Sarah paused, and finally slid her mother's costume ring off her finger. Hoggle watched her drop it in the collecting box and looked green. He'd thought he was going to get that too.

"Thank you so kindly," the hat said, sounding like a fairground barker. "Move along, please."

As they walked away, across the garden, Hoggle said, "You didn't have to give that away. He didn't tell you nothing."

"Well," Sarah said reflectively, "he said something about the way forward being sometimes the way backward. We haven't gotten anywhere so far trying to go out forward, so why don't we try walking out backward? It might work."

Hoggle's expression was skeptical, but he humored her by doing as she suggested. They walked backward through the gap in the hedge from which Sarah had last emerged, and the garden remained in peaceful silence, decorated with birdsong.

The hat was watching where they had gone. When they did not return, it chirped. "Well, what do you know! They took your advice."

"Zzzzzz," the Wise Man said, having dozed off after so much mental travail.

His hat cocked an eye down at him. "It's so stimulating being your hat."

"Zzzzzz," the Wise Man concurred.

CHAPTER VIII
A VERY LOUD VOICE

Once they had left the Wise Man, Sarah and Hoggle found that by walking forward they could move ahead. It made a nice change. Not, however, any more than a nice change, because the maze of hedges turned them left and right and back again so often that it was impossible to make any progress toward the castle. Frequently it could be seen, its spires and turrets looming in the distance above the hedges, but no matter how far and fast they walked, it remained in the distance.

Sarah was still thinking about the Wise Man. "Hoggle," she asked, "how do you tell when someone's talking sense and when he's talking rubbish?"

Hoggle shrugged impatiently. "How should I know? All I knows is we're going to get ourselves well and truly lost in this place. Let me go back."

"Not on your life. You're sticking with me now until we get there," Sarah said, wondering how much time she had left.

Hoggle said, "Huh," rather noncommittally, she thought.

Well, she still had his precious string of baubles. He wouldn't get that back until she had found Toby, and she judged that nothing would induce him to abandon her while she still had his treasure.

Alley, turning, alley, dead end, stone pillar, alley, ornamental shrub, turning, on it went, leading nowhere. Sarah wondered whether it wasn't a closed system, no exit but its entrance, that urn. It was just the kind of puzzle that Jareth would set, to waste what time she had left. But if that were so... She shuddered. Would she have the courage to go back into the urn, and down that ladder, and start over in that awful subterranean passageway?

Down, down, down, down...

She remembered the hands, and the oubliette, and that terrifying slashing machine, and Jareth in the beggar costume. She recalled a sentence that her mother had once read aloud to her from a book, as she liked to do when something caught her fancy: *Mind what you say to a beggar, it might be God in disguise*. When she saw her mother again, she would tell her: Or it might just be the King of the Goblins.

She shrugged. How could she be expected to have any respect for Jareth? He was dangerous and powerful, obviously, but he was too aware of it—a showoff, really—and mean, a cheat. He had a certain style to him, she could concede that much. He was not unattractive. But how could you respect, still less admire, someone like him? The best word she could think of to describe him was *cad*.

Alley, turning, alley... on they trudged. Hedged in as they were, they couldn't see that they were not completely alone in the maze. The head and coils of a sea serpent rode along above a hedge quite close to them, though had they actually encountered the beast they might have spotted three little pairs of goblin feet running along beneath it, and heard the grunts of goblins supporting the parts of the serpent. Several times they narrowly missed meeting a mounted goblin, with lance and flag, who had been sent out by Jareth to look for them and spent an hour galloping at random.

Hoggle was quiet for some time. Then he asked, "Why did you say that about me being your friend?"

"Because you are," she told him candidly. "You may not be much of a friend, but you're the only one I've got in this place."

Hoggle thought about it for a while. Then he said, "I ain't never been no one's friend before."

An enormous blood-curdling roar from somewhere nearby froze the two of them in their tracks.

Hoggle spun around. Pausing only to say, "Keep the stuff!" he started to run back, away from the roar.

Sarah ran after him and seized hold of his sleeve. "Wait a minute," she said angrily. "Are you my friend or not?"

While Hoggle hesitated, another air-trembling roar made up his mind for him. "No! No, I'm not. Hoggle ain't no one's friend. He looks after hisself. Like everyone does." He wriggled his sleeve free. "Hoggle is Hoggle's friend," she heard him yell, as he dashed in the opposite direction from the roaring and vanished into the maze.

"Hoggle!" Sarah called. "You coward!"

She heard another frightful roar, but stayed where she was. The monster, whatever it was, did not seem to be getting any closer to her. "Well," she said, speaking out loud to reassure herself, "I'm not going to be afraid. Things are not always what they seem in this place—that's what the Wise Man said." The sound came again, like a pride of starving lions roaring in unison. "It could be some tiny creature," Sarah told herself, "perfectly harmless… just that it happens to have a *very* loud voice…" After all, by far the loudest person at home was Toby, and he couldn't do you any harm. Was there some law she had never grasped, something to do with the smallest creatures making the loudest noise? Did dinosaurs roar? She decided not. They would have made a low growling noise. But what about ants, then? Probably they made a terrible noise, somewhere beyond the range of human hearing.

As she was not going to run away, the only alternative was to proceed in the direction they had been going, with some shred of faith that forward meant onward. And so, crossing her fingers for luck, she moved tentatively along the hedge alley.

When she reached a gap in the hedge and peered cautiously through it, she saw that things were, indeed, not always what they seemed. The roar was coming from a terrifyingly huge beast, but the animal was upside down, suspended by one leg lashed to a tree. It was roaring with pain, because four goblins were tormenting it with nipper sticks, long poles with small, fierce creatures on the end of them that bit like piranhas whenever they were given the chance.

The great beast, who was covered with shaggy, ginger hair, flailed out haplessly at the goblins, but the only result was that its body swung to and fro. That improved the game for the goblins, giving each of them the opportunity to dart in ahead of the others and get in a cruel thrust with the nipper stick before the bellowing, frantically swatting beast had completed its swing back. They were clearly having the time of their lives. They vied with each other in how soft a part of the beast's body they could reach, and how long they could hold the nipping teeth in there before they had to jump out of the way of its desperate arms. So absorbed were they that Sarah was able to leave the hedge and come closer without any risk of their noticing her.

She was appalled by the scene. "The little beasts!" she muttered to herself.

She looked around for a weapon and found some small rocks. She picked one up, took careful aim and threw it at the nearest goblin. It hit him on the head, knocking the visor of his helmet down over his eyes.

"Hey," the goblin exclaimed. "Who turned out the lights?"

He lurched around sightlessly, still swinging and thrusting out his nipper stick. The vicious creature on the end of the stick was glad to bite anything within its reach. When it made contact with another goblin, its teeth sank in.

"Ouch! Ouch!" the bitten goblin shrieked. "Hey, stop that, you."

"Stop what?" asked the first goblin, still prodding out unseeingly.

The second goblin was now under furious assault. "Aargh. Dog weed! Rat's meal!" Spitefully he retaliated by deliberately using his nipper stick.

It was the blinded goblin's turn to wail. "Help! Who's attacking me? Where are the *lights*?"

The other two goblins had paused in their tormenting of the beast. This was even better fun. They nudged each other and snickered as they watched the fight.

"Go to it!" one of them shouted.

"Get him!" yelled the other, hopping up and down in his excitement.

Sarah had armed herself with another little rock, and now she threw it. She was astonished at how accurate her aim was today. The rock hit one of the other goblins on the helmet, knocking down his visor. He staggered into his companion, and that one's visor slammed down, too, with the impact.

"Help," cried one.

"It's gone dark," squealed the other.

"What's happened?"

"Lights! Where are the lights?"

Meanwhile the first goblin, still visored and unable to see who was nipping him, decided that his only recourse was to take to his heels. Running blind, he crunched straight into the two others, who were both staggering now. His nipper stick seized its opportunity.

Sarah watched with tears of laughter in her eyes as three goblins dueled with each other, helmets over their faces, while the fourth went on cursing his wounds.

"Ouch! I'm being nipped."

"Help! Lights!"

"Ow. *Stop* it!"

"Worm rot! Teazel rash!"

The uproar faded as the pack of them pursued each other, yelling and yelping, crashing into hedges, falling over roots.

Sarah wiped her eyes, and her face became serious as she gazed at the great dangling beast. Having delivered it from its tormentors, she had half a mind to leave well enough alone and steal away. But the pity she had felt for the monster was still working in her. She approached it cautiously.

What the shaggy brute saw was another tormentor coming. It let out a terrible roar and aimed a great blow at her.

She was careful to remain just out of reach. All the same, even to stand there and face the gigantic, inverted creature took more courage than she thought she had. She remembered having read somewhere that you have to speak firmly and with confidence to wild animals. So, in her most perfect schoolteacher voice, she told it, "Now, *stop* that."

Another great roar was on its way from the depths of the monster's body, but the beast stopped in mid-roar when it heard itself thus addressed. "Murh?" it said.

Sarah clicked her tongue. "Is that any way to treat someone who's trying to help you?"

The monster still had its doubts. It tried delivering another bellow and aimed a swipe, but there was not much conviction in it.

"Stop it, do you hear?" Sarah was beginning to enjoy herself. It was a role she played well, having had plenty of time to study those who played it every day in the classroom. It was one of the parts she had liked to perform for her mother's amusement.

The monster answered, "Huh?"

"Now do you or do you not want me to get you down from that tree?"

The monster hung in there for a bit, reflecting on what its options were. It craned its neck to look up at its tethered ankle, reflected again, then turned its face to Sarah.

"Ludo—down," it said.

Its voice had become almost deferential. Its face was still fearsome, though—oxlike horns on its head, sunken eyes, an enormous jaw with a fang protruding at each end, and a broad gaping mouth that looked grim.

Sarah steeled herself to approach closely. She felt its warm breath on her face as she stood beside the beast and twisted herself down from the waist to get a look at it the right way up. What she saw surprised her. The great mouth that had looked so grim, with its turned-down corners, had actually been, of course, smiling sweetly at her. Gosh, she reflected, it must often be like that for poor Toby, when people lean over him from the pillow of his crib.

Not only was the monster grinning at her, it now blinked in a goofy sort of way, which just could mean, I-am-in-a-pickle-aren't-I-but-all-the-same-how-d'you-do-and-thanks-for-being-nice-to-me. Sarah returned a cautious smile. She was not going to credit this monster with being, uniquely in this place, what it seemed to be.

"Ludo—down," it repeated.

"Ludo," Sarah asked, "is that your name?"

"Ludo—friend."

"Uh-uh. I've had people say that to me before. So I'm not taking anything for granted. But…" She shook her head and, more to herself than to Ludo, concluded, "Your eyes are just like Merlin's."

Feeling safer now, she ruffled Ludo's ginger head, between his horns. He smiled, and sighed.

She straightened up and looked at the knot tethering Ludo's leg to the branch. It was a simple bowline, which she could release with one tug. With her hand raised, she paused, and looked down at Ludo, "I do hope you're not going to turn back into a raging monster the moment I let you down from here."

Ludo's response was another roar that made the rocks tremble.

Sarah leaped back. "I knew it! I can't trust *anyone* in this place."

But then she saw that Ludo, far from aiming a blow at her, was using his paws to rub one or two of the most tender places where the goblins had bitten him with their nipper sticks. "Ludo—hurt," he moaned.

Sarah looked more closely at him. He was covered with little bleeding wounds, under his fur. "Oh," she cried, "you poor thing!" Quickly she reached up, tugged at the rope, and released him. He hit the ground with a mighty thump.

With deep little groans, he sat himself up, and began to rub his wounded head and the sores inflicted upon him. She watched him, even now uncertain whether she should expect him to thank her or eat her.

"Goblins—mean to Ludo," he grimaced.

"Oh, I know that." She nodded, with more assurance than she felt. "They were terribly mean to you," she told Ludo. She moved closer to him and patted his arm. "But it's all right now."

He sniffled, still rubbing. Then his face broke into the most endearing big dumb smile she had ever seen, bigger and dumber even than in any cartoon. "Friend!" Ludo declared.

"That's right, Ludo. I'm Sarah."

"Sarah—friend."

"Yes, I am." She couldn't smile big and dumb like that, but she gave him the best she could do. "And," she added, "I want to ask a favor of you, Ludo."

"Huh?"

"I have to get to the castle at the center of the Labyrinth. Do you know the way there?"

Ludo shook his great head, still beaming at her.

Sarah sighed, and her shoulders sagged. "You don't know the way either?"

Again, he shook his head, with a small frown of apology.

"I wonder if anyone knows how to get through the Labyrinth."

Sarah rested her chin in her hand, philosophically. He was a dear monster, and likely to prove much more trustworthy than that runty, cowardly pipsqueak, but she could have done with a guide. Well, if no one was going to help her, she would find out what she could do on her own.

She stood up. Ludo stood with her, massively towering over her. He may be no guide, she thought, but it's nice to have him on my side.

CHAPTER IX
ANOTHER DOOR OPENS

Sarah walked past the hanging tree. Ludo, wincing with the soreness of his nipped body, followed.

Behind the tree, two high doorways had appeared, set into a stone wall that seemed to be part of a rough forest hedge. On each door was an iron knocker.

"Well, look at these," she remarked, glad to have a companion again. It was more fun than talking to herself.

They approached the doorways and looked more closely at the knockers. Each had the form of a repulsive face, with a ring set in it. The knocker to her left had the ring coming out of its ears. The one on the right held the ring in its mouth.

She looked from one to the other. Which to choose? She always found choices hard to make; if there were two kinds of cake at a birthday party, she would contrive to have a bit of each, at a decent interval, naturally, and hoping that no one noticed. Now she looked around the glade, to see if there was some other way past this wall. There wasn't, and so she examined the knockers. "Well, Ludo," she asked, "which one of these two ugly characters shall we choose?"

"It's very rude to stare," said the first knocker, the one with the ring set in its ears.

Sarah jumped, still not accustomed to the habit that normally inarticulate things had, in the Labyrinth, of speaking their minds.

"I'm sorry," she said, though she felt that she was scarcely to blame for assuming that a door knocker would have no mind to speak, let alone blunt opinions on acceptable social behavior. "I was just wondering which door to choose, that's all."

"What?" the first knocker asked.

Sarah was about to reply that, where she came from, to say "What?" was thought just as rude as staring. But before she could open her mouth, she heard a mumbling noise from behind her.

It was the second knocker, with the ring in its mouth. It said something like "Mmm gli m g any."

"Don't talk with your mouth full," the first knocker said primly.

"Ker glimpfwrt mble mble mble…"

Sarah addressed the second knocker: "I don't understand what you're saying." Then she realized what the problem was. "Ah," she said, "wait a moment."

"What was that?" the first knocker inquired.

Sarah took hold of the ring in the second knocker's mouth and pulled. It came away easily. The face looked tremendously relieved. It exercised the muscles around its jaw and chin with evident pleasure.

"It's so good to get that thing out," it sighed.

"What were you saying?" Sarah asked.

The first knocker, behind her, said, "Huh?"

The second knocker nodded at the first. "I said it's no good talking to him. Oh, dear me, no. He's deaf as a post, that one, I can tell you."

The first knocker said, "Mumble, mumble, mumble, that's you. You're a wonderful conversational companion, I must say."

"*YOU* SHOULD TALK!" the second knocker yelled back. "ALL YOU DO IS MOAN!"

"It's no good," the first knocker said, in a matter-of-fact voice. "I can't hear you."

Sarah looked at the second knocker. "Where do these doors lead?" she asked it.

"What?" asked the first knocker.

"Search me," the second one answered her. "We're just the knockers."

"Oh," Sarah said, reflecting that she ought to have known better than to expect a simple answer.

Well, she had to try either one door or the other. She chose the second one. Having engaged in discourse with it, however slightly, she felt it would somehow have been discourteous to turn her back and choose its neighbor. On the other hand, it could be that the knockers would prefer their doors not to be opened. She shouldn't take it for granted that the knockers would like people to make use of them. Every *either* had its *or*. If she weighed the implications of every alternative, would she ever get to make a choice at all? When one door opens, so does another one.

She had committed herself to the second door by now, with her hands against it, so she went ahead and pushed. It didn't budge. She pushed harder. She leaned her shoulder against the door. It was as solid as the wall it was set in. She thought of asking Ludo to help her. His gigantic bulk would surely open the door.

But she wasn't sure it was the right door to choose, and so, instead, she asked another question. "How do we get through?"

"Huh?" said the first knocker.

The second one, with an arch smile, replied, "Knock and the door will open."

"Ah." She looked at the ring she held, and went to put it back in the second knocker's mouth.

He made a face. "Uh-uh, I don't want that thing back in my mouth." And he clamped his lips tightly shut, and refused to open them even when she put the ring against his mouth.

"Oh, come on," Sarah said encouragingly. "I want to knock."

He shook his head stubbornly.

"Hmmm," commented the first knocker, morosely as usual. "Doesn't want the ring back in his mouth. Can't say as I blame him."

"Then," Sarah said, putting down the ring, "I'm afraid I'll have to bother you instead." She walked over to the first knocker and took hold of its ring.

"Ow! Ooh," the first knocker protested.

Sarah took no notice. She knocked twice upon the heavy door. It swung open.

Cautiously, she put her head through the doorway, to see what was beyond. She heard giggles, splutters of suppressed laughter, honks and hoots. Instinctively she started to grin herself, and went farther through the doorway. She turned, waiting for Ludo to follow her. He remained in the doorway, shaking his head.

"Come on, Ludo."

He shook his head again.

"Well," she thought, "it can't do any harm to see where this might lead." She would come back for Ludo if she spotted the castle.

She was in a sunlit forest, with clumps and banks of flowers, daisy-decked hillocks, dingles and dells, shady trees all around. The laughter was infectious. Giggling, she looked hard for the creatures who were enjoying all this merriment. All she could see were the forest plants. "Who is it?" she called out, chuckling.

From right behind her came a laughing snort. She spun around and saw a tree's branch moving to cover a hollow in its trunk that just might have been its mouth. "It was the tree," she declared. "Tree, wasn't it you?"

That sparked off a tinkle of giggles at her feet. She looked down and saw a cluster of bluebells shivering and shaking together with amusement.

"Oh, look!" she exclaimed, falling to her knees and giggling with them. They were beside themselves with hilarity now.

The tree above her could hold it in no longer. It exploded in a bellow of mirth. Sarah threw her head back and joined in.

It was the signal for a general outburst. A tree stump nearby was laughing in a deep, cracked voice. Birds on a branch were hopping and cackling. Another tree was rocking. Ferns waved about, squirrels and mice peeped from their holes with tears in their eyes.

Sarah was helpless with laughing. Catching a breath, she panted, "What are we laughing at?"

"I don't know!" the tree above her roared. "Ha-ha-ha-ha!"

The whole forest shook. Even the grass on the ground was trembling.

Sarah was feeling faint. She sat down. "Oh… please… please, I must stop." She clutched her sides.

In response, the laughter around her redoubled. It reached a pitch of hysterical shrillness.

"I've never laughed so much in my life," Sarah gasped, flat on her back.

Birds convulsed with mirth fell out of the trees and hit the ground headfirst. She saw their eyes were mad, with pinprick pupils. Other creatures came screaming from under the roots of trees, and as they approached her she managed to sit up, alarmed by their sinister gaping mouths and crazy eyes.

Still laughing, she moaned, "Oh, please, please! I must stop."

"She can't stop!" the tree howled, and the whole forest screeched in reply.

She got to her feet. Her body and mouth were shaking uncontrollably, but her eyes were haggard. "Stop!" she whispered. "Stop!" She staggered back toward the open doorway and collapsed.

Shrieking hysteria applauded that.

She raised her head. She could see Ludo just outside the door, and held up her hand for help. He looked very uneasy and wouldn't come inside the door, but he held his arm out toward her, and nodded his great head in encouragement. Her eyes fixed on him, she dragged herself across the last few yards, until he could bend down, pick her up, take her outside, and shut the door.

The laughter stopped dead. The breeze in the leaves of the maze outside was the sweetest sound she'd ever heard.

It took her some time to recover. Ludo watched over her anxiously. When she stood up, sniffed, and gave him a small smile, he said, "Ludo—glad."

"Sarah—glad," she answered, and ruffled his head.

There was nothing for it but to try the other door. She walked across to it, picking up the ring.

"I'm sorry," she said, and pushed the ring against the knocker's lips. He pursed his mouth and resisted her.

"Oh, come on," she said, and tried again. The knocker frowned and squeezed his lips together even more tightly.

Then she had an idea. With her finger and her thumb, she squeezed the knocker's nose. He held out for a while, scowling more and more fiercely, but in the end he had to open his mouth for breath. "Damn!" he gasped.

In a flash, she had the ring back in his mouth, and knocked on the door.

He was protesting. "Kgrmpf. Mble. Mble. Mble. Grmfff."

"Sorry," Sarah said. "I had to do it."

"That's all right," the first knocker told her. "He's used to it."

The door swung open to reveal a forbidding forest. On this side of the wall they were in sunshine, but through the doorway was a dismal and brooding prospect.

Ludo was growling and trying to draw back, but Sarah was not going in without him this time. "Come on," she said, and braced herself. "There's no other way we can go. Except back where we came from, and I'm not doing that."

She stepped through the doorway and waited for Ludo to join her. He followed her, reluctantly. The door swung shut of its own accord, with a resounding thud. The echo lasted a long time.

Sarah shivered. The sky was the color of cast iron, and the forest plants looked shriveled, as though the sun had never shone on them since their first day on earth. She felt terribly dispirited after just a minute in this place, and she looked for Ludo to hearten her. His expression was unhappier than her own.

"Oh, come on, Ludo," she said, trying to sound cheerful. "Fancy a great thing like you being so scared."

Ludo shook his head. "Not—good."

She shrugged, with a heavy heart, turned around again, and wondered which way to go. A path ran in front of her into the forest, but how could anyone take it for granted that a path was the way you wanted to go? "I don't know which way the castle is," she said. Again she looked at Ludo, hoping that from his height he would be able to see it, but he had his head sunk resolutely on his chest and took no notice. She tried standing on tiptoe. That was no good.

Nothing was any good. She felt a tear of despair rim her eye and brushed it irritably away. "There's nothing to be scared of," she said, and felt she had to take some initiative, if only to persuade Ludo to buck up.

She peered up into the branches of a tree. What she did not see, behind her, was that the earth opened up beneath Ludo and swallowed him into a great hole. He had no time to utter more than the first tremor of a roar before the earth closed again above his head.

"Maybe I could climb up there," Sarah was saying. "Then I must be able to see the way to the castle."

She took hold of the lowest branch and put her weight on it. It snapped off in her hand, with a dry crack like china, and before she could register that it was dead the whole tree collapsed. Lying before her she saw a pile not of dead wood but of bones. The thing she was holding was a bone. With a shudder she threw it away. There was a dry, rustling noise going on all around, and in dismay she saw the whole forest was collapsing, like a series of dinosaur skeletons.

One bone tree after the other clattered to the ground, each bringing down the next, like dominoes, until the entire landscape had been reduced to heaps of bones, all jumbled together. And Sarah knew it was all her fault, the destruction of this delicate balance. She had snapped off the branch. It was too much to bear. She burst out weeping and sank to the ground. She couldn't do anything right. It was all hopeless. Quite hopeless.

She cried and cried, with her hands over her face. Eventually she looked to see if Ludo was crying, too. "Ludo?" She looked all around her. He wasn't there. Distractedly, she inspected the bones on the ground to see if any had ginger fur on them.

"Ludo!" She rushed around the spot where the two of them had been, looking in a panic for any sign of him. She saw none. Above, the sky had grown even darker and more miserable. "*Ludo!*" she screamed, feeling utterly alone in this desolate bonescape. "Where are you? What's going on?"

She ran, to get away, anywhere. If she stayed there she would be bones herself. She ran through the heaps of bones and into another part of the forest, also grim. Huge gnarled roots stretched across the path. The trees had trunks like tight fists. Fallen branches and dead leaves covered the earth. Here and there a brief vista between the trees offered a way on, but along each one that she took cobwebs clothed her face. From clumps of ferns, clouds of dark moths flitted up at her. "What's going on?" she whimpered as she ran.

The forest got darker as she ran deeper into it. She stumbled into a glade above which the trees were so close that she could not see her feet in the darkness. Still she ran, until a terrifying, bright, savage figure leaped out in front of her.

"Yeah!" it screeched. "What's going on?"

Sarah's mouth and eyes formed circles. She screamed.

CHAPTER X
NO PROBLEM

Hoggle was hoggling around the hedge maze still, minding his own business, and most of all minding that that girl had gotten his jewels. He'd tried to please both her and Jareth, and that's what you got for trying to please everyone. No baubles.

When Sarah screamed, he heard her. It stopped him in his tracks, which were heading for the start of the Labyrinth. He listened, heard a second scream, wrestled with his rudimentary conscience, came to a decision, and began to run in her direction. He knew his way around this place better than the stupid goblins in the castle. "I'm coming, missy," he shouted.

He galloped around the corner straight into a pair of knees.

Jareth was wearing his cloak and looking quite handsomely fiendish. "Well," he said pleasantly, "if it isn't you."

"It isn't me," Hoggle told him, trembling.

"And where are *you* going, hmm?"

"Ah…" Hoggle was staring at Jareth's boots. "Ah…," he said in a different tone of voice, to hold his audience's attention. Then he spent a little while scratching his backside, suggesting that a person can't be expected to answer a question while he's plagued with an itch.

Jareth was content to wait, with a smile on his lips.

"Er…" At last Hoggle came up with it. "The little missy, she give me the slip… er… but I just hears her now…"

Jareth's eyes narrowed.

"So I'm… er… er, I'm going to fetch her and then lead her straight back to the beginning. Just like you told me." He wished the King of the Goblins would kick him, or pelt him with slugs, or do anything, anything but smile that nerve-racking, pleasant smile.

"I see," Jareth nodded. "I thought for a moment you were running to help her. But no, you wouldn't. Not after my warnings. That would be stupid."

"Ha-ha," Hoggle agreed, with a trembling heart. "Oh, ha-ha-ha. Stupid? You bet it would be stupid. *Me?* Help *her?* After your warnings?"

Jareth elegantly inclined his head to examine Hoggle's belt. "Oh, dear," he said, seeming concerned, "poor Hoghead!"

"Hoggle," Hoggle growled.

"I just noticed that your lovely jewels are missing."

"Uh…" Hoggle looked down at his sadly unadorned belt. "Oh, yes. So they are. My lovely jewels. Missing. There now. Better find 'em, eh? But first," he promised in a profoundly reliable voice, "I'm off to fetch the little missy back to the beginning of the Labyrinth." He thought of trying to wink, but decided not to. "Just like we planned," he said, and started to march obediently away.

"Wait," Jareth told him.

Hoggle froze. His eyes closed.

"I have a better plan, Hoggle. Give her this."

With a wave of his left hand, Jareth produced a bubble from the air. In his hand it became a crystal ball. He waited for Hoggle to turn around and tossed it to him. Hoggle caught it. It had become a peach. Hoggle looked at it, dumbfounded. "Wha—what is it?"

"A present."

Hoggle's eyebrows beetled. "It… it ain't going to harm the little missy, is it?" he asked slowly.

"Oh." Jareth placed his hand over his heart. "Now, why the concern?"

Hoggle pursed his lips. "Just… curious."

"Give it to her, Hoggle. That's all you have to do. And all you have to know."

Hoggle was torn between fearful obedience, which was familiar to him, and affection, to which he could not have put a name. "I…" He stood more erect. "I won't do nothing to harm her." He reckoned that such a moment of defiance might have earned him a pint of earwigs down his breeches, at least.

Instead, Jareth replied with that pleasant smile that by now was like broken glass on Hoggle's nerves. "Come, come, come, Hogbrain," the Goblin King laughed teasingly, "I'm surprised at you. Losing your ugly head over a *girl*."

"I ain't lost my head," Hoggle scowled.

"You don't imagine that a young girl could ever *like* a repulsive little scab like you, do you?"

Hoggle was stung. "She said we was…" He stopped himself in mid-blurt, but it was too late.

Jareth gave him a coy, sideways grin. "What? Bosom companions? Was that it, Piggle? Piggly-Wiggly? Friends, are you?"

Hoggle, red-faced, was blinking at his boots again. "Don't matter," he muttered.

Jareth's voice came back crisply. "You give her that, Hoggle, or I'll have you tipped straight into the Bog of Eternal Stench before you can blink."

In miserable obedience, Hoggle nodded. "Yes."

He had started to hurry on his way, assuming the interview was over, when he heard Jareth's voice again. He stopped, rigid, not daring to turn around.

"I'll tell you what." Jareth had his head back and was looking down his nose at Hoggle. "If she ever kisses you—I'll turn you into a prince."

Hoggle knew there was going to be a catch. "You will?"

There was a catch. "Prince of the Land of Stench."

Jareth thought that was a capital joke. He was still laughing as he disappeared.

Hoggle remained standing still, staring at the peach in his hand. His face registered several emotions at once. Amusement was not among them.

The bright, savage figure that had leaped out in front of Sarah was a Firey, and the Fireys are *wild*. Are they ever. They are wild about how wild they are.

She screamed a second time and shrank away from the creature, hands folded across herself. It was a bit like a scrawny fox, with a long snout that opened very wide, and a bushy tail. Its fur was red-pink-purplish. It walked, or rather bounded, on two chickenlike legs. Its staring eyes were blue, with red pupils. It had very long fingers, which seemed to be perpetually drumming.

"What's happening?" it demanded.

She shook her head and opened her mouth to frame some sort of answer, but all that came out was a sob.

"Now cut that out right now, you hear?" the Firey told her.

"Yeah," agreed another one from behind her, making her start around in fright. "That ain't gonna do no good."

"No, sir!" hollered a third one, prancing from the trees and leering wildly at her.

"No, sir." A fourth one appeared.

And a fifth. "Hey!" it said to her, rousingly, "Come *on*, now."

She looked around at them all in great alarm. "What do you want?"

"Wa-*hoo!*" one replied, rapping out a fast rhythm with his fingers on a rock.

"Hoot!" another said, setting up a cross-rhythm.

"What, us?" asked a third.

Sarah nodded.

"Why, we're just after havin' ourselves a good time."

"Oh," Sarah said, confused. "I see."

They all slapped their sides at her demure reply and laughed maniacally. One let out a whoop and hit his hand on a log.

"She *sees!*" it howled.

"Yeeeahhh!"

"Hey-*ey!*"

"You can't stick around like that," one told her.

"No," said another. "You gotta shake it loose a bit."

"Yeahhh. Quit crying. Let it all hang *out.*"

They leaped around, hooting and clapping. One struck his finger on the ground and it ignited, like a match. He used it to light a bonfire, then blew his finger out nonchalantly.

Sarah was still timidly backing away.

"Oh, *yeah.* What you need is a little mess-around."

"Yes, sir!"

A Firey jumped over a pair of tree stumps and started using them as drums. The rest broke into an up-tempo dance number, clicking and drumming their fingers as they circled around her.

Sarah watched in astonishment, standing near the bonfire. She couldn't have fled if she'd wanted to, with them capering all around her, but in any case she was rooted to the spot by their antics.

She was horrified to see one of the Fireys pluck out his eyes, shake them like dice, and throw them. "Yeah," the others all cheered, crowding around to look at them. "Snake eyes!" Then the owner of the eyes snatched them up, tossed them in the air like peanuts, and caught them in his eye sockets. The rest were hooting and dancing and clapping.

As though to outdo the first, another Firey took his head off his shoulders and threw it in the air. It was kicked and headed around like a soccer ball. Another took his leg off, and with a delicate chip shot hit the head back onto its body. They all cackled and slapped their thighs. The drummer went wild.

Meanwhile, the rest crowded around Sarah and tried to persuade her to join in the dance. After seeing their wild pastimes, she was shy and nervous of them. But she thought she had their number now— just crazy good-timers, out of their skulls—and she was no longer frightened, not even when one tried to lift her head from her shoulders.

"Hey!" she protested. "Ouch!"

"It don't come off!" the Firey exclaimed.

"*What?*" The rest were astonished, and they all gathered around in the attempt to decapitate her.

"Ow!" she said, more sternly. "Stop it!"

"You're right! It's fixed on!"

"Of course it's *fixed* on," she told them.

"Where you goin' with a head like that, lady?"

"Well, I'm… oh!" The hopelessness of her predicament flooded back, and she started to sob again. She was missing Ludo terribly, and Hoggle, too.

"Hey! Now what's up, little lady?"

Sarah hiccupped. "Oh! I'm trying to get to Jareth's castle at the center of this Labyrinth…"

"Holy Mo!"

"You *sure* you know what you're doin', lady?"

"Yes," Sarah said firmly.

"Well, hot dog! How *about* that!"

The drummer shouted, "She *knows* what she's doin'," and he gave her a drumroll on the tree stumps.

"Yeah," the others said, grinning and bopping.

"But I've only got a few hours left," Sarah told them. She wondered how few.

The Fireys whistled and grinned at each other.

"Well, that ain't *no* problem."

Sarah looked up at them through her tears, with a glint of hope in her eyes. "Isn't it?"

"Why, shoot! No!"

"We'll take you there."

"Yeah," another squawked wildly, waving his fingers above his head. "How about us comin' *along* a little, hey?"

The rest cavorted in a frenzy of excitement, hooting and screeching.

"A castle, oh, wow!"

"Well," Sarah said doubtfully, "it's kind of you, but…"

"You think we're just *too wild*?" The Firey's head rose up from his shoulders as he spoke, and he had to grab it in his hands and press it back into place.

The drummer did a big roll. "Why, *shoot*. We ain't *that* wild."

"Oh, yes, we are," another called. "Hey!" He formed himself into the shape of an ostrich, ran two steps, and exploded. As he put his pieces together again, the rest howled and clapped.

"Cool, man!"

"Now look, little lady, you can't just go walkin' through this place on your ownsome."

Sarah sniffed sadly. "Well, I did have a friend just—"

"Hey! Fellow with clothes on, right?"

"Hoggle?"

"That Hoggle, yeah! Oh, wow! Everyone around these parts knows Hoggle."

"Really?" Sarah asked.

"Sure. Hog and me, we're like that." The Firey crossed his fingers.

"Oh. Well…"

Before she could say any more, Sarah felt herself being propelled along by the Fireys. All she could see ahead of them was a rocky wilderness.

"Now the castle's just down along around this way," one assured her.

"Are you sure you *know* how to get to the center of the Labyrinth?" she asked nervously. She had precious little time to waste, and she thought she would have preferred to be left to find her own way. But there was no escaping the Fireys, who had hold of her clothes in their long fingers and were hopping enthusiastically along with her in tow.

"Do *we* know how to get to the center of the Labyrinth!"

They all burst out laughing. Their heads flew up in the air, and their arms had to detach themselves to catch the heads.

"Why, lady!" one screeched. "We may be *wild* but we sure know where we're goin'."

"Yeahhh!" the rest concurred.

"You wanna go to the castle? We're *takin'* you to the castle. Ain't we just doin' that thing?"

"Yeeeahhh!"

"So you come on along with us, little lady, and you ain't gonna have *no* problem."

Jareth was watching Sarah from the castle. In his crystal he saw her distraught face looking around for a way to escape.

He held Toby up in front of his sister's picture. "Look, Sarah," he murmured. "Is this what you're trying to find?"

Toby gaped at Sarah's face in the crystal. He held a hand out to touch it.

Jareth chuckled to himself and put his arms around Toby. "So much trouble for such a little thing," Jareth said, shaking his head. He looked at Toby's puzzled face. "But not for long. Soon she'll forget all about you, my fine fellow. Just as soon as Hoggle gives her my present. She'll forget—everything."

CHAPTER XI
WINDOWS IN THE WILDERNESS

The Fireys were hauling Sarah along as though she were a reluctant donkey. She was certainly reluctant. She could not see the castle anywhere, and when she asked them how far away it was they answered with whoops and cackles. The clock was ticking toward thirteen all the time. So perhaps she was indeed a donkey for having got herself into this mess.

She tried to figure out where she should have made a different choice. It was impossible. Suppose she had not approached Hoggle, right at the start, but walked the other way around that great wall? Might she not, by now, be back home, with Toby safe in his crib? Perhaps. How would she know? What evidence had she been given that any of her choices were the right ones? If there *were* right ones; if it wasn't all a cruel hoax by which Jareth tormented her with the illusion that Toby could be rescued.

She blinked back rising tears. She would not start that again. If she hadn't been a crybaby, perhaps these creatures she was with now would have left her alone.

She concentrated on what could be evidence, however flimsy, that she had gotten some things right. Her brief friendship with Ludo, poor Ludo—that couldn't be meaningless, could it? The happy, goofy smile he'd given her when she had rescued him—was that a gratuitous event in a story with no ending? Even Hoggle, flawed character though he was, had unwittingly helped her to find out that she was capable of doing more than she had known. To have gotten this far at all, in spite of the hideous traps Jareth had set for her—surely that was some kind of evidence in her favor?

Perhaps. But it would mean nothing at all unless she could get to Toby in time, and save him from being turned into a goblin. She had to get away from this bunch, who were just passing the time—her time.

"Hey! Ain't that it over there?" one yelled.

"Noo-h," another said. "That's just a rock."

"How 'bout *that?* That a castle?"

"Noo-oh, that's just the stump of an ol' tree."

"Well," shrieked another of them, "how 'bout *that?* That got to be a castle." He was pointing at a pond.

"Nohow," the wiser one said. "A castle's got windows and all that."

An eel popped its head above the surface of the pond and looked at them. The effect was as though they'd struck oil.

"It *is* a castle."

"Doggone," conceded the wiser one. "Well, whaddya know? We must be there."

"Ye-eaahh!"

"Hey!"

"Wow-*eee!*"

Sarah looked coolly at their whoopings and leapings. "That's not the castle," she told them.

"It got windows. That ol' eel must've looked outa *somethin'*."

"Well," Sarah answered, "it's not the castle I have to find. Please let me go now."

"Now, you," the eel piped. "What're you doing?"

"We're just havin' ourselves a good old time."

They were capering about, slapping their thighs.

"Hey, eel. You a *castle?*"

"No, I ain't," the eel trilled tartly. "Now get along."

"Hey, eel. So why you got windows?"

"So's I can tell *you* to scat," the eel replied, and vanished with aplomb and a plop.

"Hot dog!" They were unaccountably delighted with everything that happened. Setback or success, it made no difference.

"Please," Sarah said, "I want to go."

"Ain't you havin' a good time?"

"Yes," she lied politely. "But I must get to the castle."

"We *nearly* found it for you."

"It did have windows. Well, one, anyway."

"We want to help you."

"Yeah! 'Cause we like you."

Sarah sighed. "But you've got no more idea of where the castle is than I have."

"We have too!"

"No you haven't."

"It's just over this here hill."

"Yeah, you tell her."

"Come on! What we waiting for?"

Bopping and raving, they dragged Sarah on through the wilderness, and on, until even they began to look exhausted and a little downcast.

As for Sarah, her body was wilting and her spirit was exasperated.

"These castles are sure hard to find."

"Maybe it's a small one," another suggested.

"Uh-*huh*. Good thinkin'."

Whereupon they all started to pick up little stones and peer beneath them.

"No," Sarah told them wearily. "Castles are big things."

"Maybe it's over the hill," one said to another. "Just have a look-see if you can spot the *castle* from up there." He pointed to a fir tree.

"Sure thing!" said the other.

He took his head off and ran, bouncing it. When he arrived at the tree, he tossed his head neatly onto the topmost branches.

"Can you see the castle?"

"Yeah," the elevated head answered. "I can see the *castle!*"

"What does it look like?" asked Sarah suspiciously.

"Well, it looks kinda like… er… like a… *like a hippopotamus!*"

"Wow!"

"That's some castle."

"We're as good as there. Come on!"

"Wait for me," called out the head, while his body scrambled to reach him.

"I'm going back," Sarah announced.

"Lady! You *heard* him say he sees the castle."

"A big one!"

"Like a hippopopotamus… mus."

They were whooping and jigging around so frenetically that she thought she might be able to slip away from them without being noticed. She walked slowly, letting them all get on ahead of her. Then she turned and quietly walked back in the direction from which they had come. Of course, they were at her side again in an instant, and they all toiled on through the wilderness together.

Sarah was aiming to get back to where they had started, but then she realized the futility of that, since she would have no idea where to go next. She wondered what was the point of doing anything. She might as well go this way, or that, or stand still, or cry. Maybe just havin' yourself a good time was the best anyone could hope for.

She shook her head and halted. Whatever the point was, all this was beside it. She could do nothing until she had rid herself of the Fireys. As they jigged happily about her, she looked around the wilderness for an idea. Any idea.

She noticed, in the distance and to one side of them, a wooded bluff. She knew what she had to do.

She turned and addressed the Fireys. "Wait a minute. None of you knows where the castle is. You don't even know what a castle looks like."

"Just 'cause we're *wild* don't mean we don't know what a castle is."

"We ain't stupid, we're just *wild*."

"Yeah, *wild*," they all agreed enthusiastically.

She waited.

As she anticipated, one of them showed how wild he was by picking up his head and tossing it in the air. As it came down, Sarah grabbed it, and threw it as far away as she could.

"Hey. That's *his* head, lady."

Two more heads had leaped up to see where the first one had gone. Sarah grabbed them too, and hurled them in different directions.

"That's *my* head!" one of the heads protested as it flew through the air.

Pandemonium broke out.

"Hey, *wait* a minute."

"Lady, what are you *doing?*"

"You threw *their* heads!"

"Yeah, you're only allowed to throw your *own* head, right?"

While trunks were pursuing heads, getting the wrong ones and chucking them around, Sarah bolted. She made for the bluff.

"Stop her, someone!"

"We gotta take *your* head off now."

"Yeah, we get to throw your head *around*."

"You can't quit now."

"I'll take her head off."

"Hey, little lady!"

"Hey there, come back."

"We gotta *help* you."

"Come on, everybody!"

They gave chase and gained on her, but her initial advantage got her to the bluff before they had caught up. Slipping between trees, ahead of her she saw a crevice in a high rockface, and sprinted into it. She found herself in an alleyway running mazily through the rock. As she ran on, she heard the Fireys' voices behind her, echoing. She had hoped she'd shaken them off.

"Hey, lady, you want to take your head off, don't you?"

"Sure she does!"

"It's lots of fun."

She ran on, oblivious, until the alleyway reached a dead end. Her eye ran up the rockface wall patterned with mosses and lichens, and saw no holds for climbing. At the top, the wall had been crenellated, like the battlements of an old fortress.

She heard them come around the last bend, behind her. There was no escaping them.

"There she is!"

"Hey, lady, we found another castle!"

"Like a lunchbox!"

"No, like a wheelbarrow!"

"Wow-*eee!*"

"Wait, lady!"

Sarah closed her eyes.

Something tickled her nose. She opened her eyes and saw a rope. She threw her head back. Leaning over the parapet, high above, was a face. Hoggle's face.

"Grab it!" he called down to her.

She grabbed it. Hoggle hauled. The Fireys dove at her. They were too late by inches. They leaped up, snatching at her feet. She felt fingers brush her shoes.

"Hey, don't you want to look like us?"

"Come on, take off your head!"

"Off with her head!"

"Get a saw."

"It won't hurt."

Hoggle hauled on. Heads began to fly up beside her.

"Now come on down, lady."

"Come on—we'll let you play if you take off your arm."

"How about a leg?"

"An ear! Just take off your ear, lady. You don't *need* two."

One after another the heads rose beside her, yammered, and fell.

"We want to *help* you."

"Ain't we a-showin' you a *good* time?"

"Yeah! You come down and strut your stuff."

"Let it all hang out, little lady."

"Aw, c'mon, it's fun. Let's look for somethin' *else.*"

Hoggle had hauled her to the top. He helped her clamber over the battlements and brushed his hand at the flying heads as if they were pestering flies. "Shoo!" he bade them. "Go away."

Sarah was looking around, laughing in her relief. They were standing on top of a turret. To either side of them the stone platform of the Great Goblin Wall ran as far as she could see, rising and falling, turning, crenellated all the way, turreted at regular intervals.

She turned to face him. "Hoggle!" she said warmly.

He ignored her, continuing to beat his hands at the last few despondent heads that rose up beyond the battlements. "Down!" he barked at them. "Go on, get away with you."

When there were no more heads, he had to turn back to face Sarah, who was still beaming at him. The look he returned was as grumpy as ever, but it could not puncture the deep, affectionate gratitude she felt. He kept his eyes lowered, maybe checking his baubles, which she had strung from her belt. On his own belt hung a pouch in which he carried the peach Jareth had given him.

She held out her arms. "You've come back to help me. Thank you, Hoggle." She caught hold of him and leaned over toward his face.

"No!" he wailed, and tried to brush her off like one of the flying heads. "No! Don't *kiss* me!"

But she had done it, and the earth moved beneath them.

CHAPTER XII
AND NO BIRDS SING

The paving stones on which they were standing flipped open like trapdoors and precipitated them into a dark chute. They skidded helplessly down it.

To have gotten this far had required Sarah to be persistent in threading her way through the mazes and in resolving paradoxes. That was nothing, Hoggle would have told her, had he not been skating down the chute on his back, waving his arms and legs in the air like an unhinged wood louse. Jareth was King of the Castle, and he would tolerate no display of emotion here, no gesture of friendship or sentimentality. With her kiss, Sarah had fulfilled Jareth's menacing promise to Hoggle—that Hoggle would become "Prince of the Land of Stench."

Everyone in Jareth's realm was an island. If you did something for someone else, it was never an act of kindness but of calculation, an investment that would return a percentage when you called on it. The verb "to give" was considered obscene, and was scrawled on lavatory walls. The verb "to love" connoted nothing but desire. You stood on your own two feet, and if you could stand on somebody else's feet at the same time and reach higher in the fruit tree, you were doing all right, which was better than doing good. How much envy you could command from others was the measure of your success. Everyone in the castle envied Jareth. All his questions were answered. He was going to keep things this way.

The chute skittered them down to a sort of vent, and they tumbled out of it onto a narrow ledge, about halfway up the immense inside face of the Great Goblin Wall. Hoggle came out first, landing sideways, and as a result he rolled over the edge. Sarah, arriving just behind him, luckily landed on her feet. Thrown forward onto her hands and knees, she was just able to grab Hoggle's hand before he dropped.

Swinging dizzily above the sheer fall, Hoggle squealed for a moment. Then he stopped. A more potent emotion than fear was working on him, particularly on his bulbous nose. He wrinkled it. Then he shut his eyes and said with a puckered mouth, "Urrrggh!"

Sarah's reaction was similar. In spite of their precarious perch, all her attention was concentrated on her sense of smell. Nothing like it had ever assailed her, nothing had even suggested that such a stink could be generated within the universe.

"Urrrrggggh!" Hoggle groaned. "Blech!"

"What *is* it?" Sarah asked, agonized.

The face that Hoggle turned back up to Sarah's was haggard. "It's...," he gasped. "It's... the... Bog... of...," he swallowed, "...of Eternal Stench."

She remembered Jareth's threat to Hoggle, in that terrible passageway, and Hoggle's explanation to her, later on, that should one drop of that quagmire ever stain you it could never be washed away, nor would the stink ever abate. At the time she had not taken it seriously.

She did now.

"Urghh!" she moaned. "I've never smelled anything... It's like... like... urgghhh!"

"It doesn't matter what it's *like*," Hoggle told her sharply. "It is the Bog of Eternal Stench." And in quite a small voice, so that he did not have to inhale deeply, he added, "Help."

She recalled that she was holding Hoggle up. Straightening her knees, she managed to haul him alongside her, as he had recently hauled her on the rope.

Far below them, at the foot of the wall, was a vast mire. It was darkish khaki in color. All across its surface, bubbles of fetid air, having forced their way up through the viscous sludge, were gently popping. As they popped they cast a little spray of filth in a ring around them, and it took several minutes for the droplets to settle back again.

The noise was indescribably disgusting. The seldom used adjective *borborygmus* is inadequate. Other commentators have been driven to the coinage *evisceral*, after finding that *glairy* or *mucilaginous* did not arouse in their reader anything like the appropriate degree of revulsion.

But if it is scarcely possible to describe the noise, what hope is there of finding in any dictionary an adjective for the smell? One writer tackled the problem thus: "If you call to mind the three worst stinks that have ever molested you, sensitive-nostriled reader, imagine them raised to the power of seven, then intensively distilled into a small but curiously powerful pump held an inch away from your face and driven by a fan, you ought not to have reached the end of this sentence for the tears in your eyes, such is the iniquity of that odor."

The ledge on which Sarah and Hoggle were standing was narrow, but the pathway it offered in either direction along the wall was narrower yet. Not only that; Sarah could see that many stones in the ledge were insecure, just balanced on each other, the mortar perished. The thought of going ten steps along it was frightening, let alone going however far around the wall it ran before it offered some escape. She could not see the end of it in either direction. Very probably it would have no end at all, but just bring you back here again. Not that you would have the slightest hope of getting that far before it crumbled beneath you. Even as Sarah and Hoggle stood wondering which way to try, some small stones under their feet broke off and went cascading down into the mire far below.

Hoggle was looking far from grateful for being saved by Sarah. He scowled up at her. "What did you go and do that for?"

"What, recue you?" She was bewildered.

"No. You *kissed* me."

She looked at him. "Don't pretend to be so hard. You came back to help me. Don't deny it. You *are* my friend."

He blew out his cheeks. "Did not. Am not. I just come to get me property back, that you filched from me." He reached down and took hold of the peach. "And… to, er… to give you… uh, give you…"

"Give me what?"

Hoggle shifted his weight onto his other foot, nervously. It was enough. The stone on which he was standing gave way, and fell. Others beside it, which had been supported by it, followed. Then the entire section of the ledge broke off, and Hoggle went down with it, snatching uselessly at a piece of rock that came away in his hand.

Too late, Sarah tried to grab him. Off balance, she teetered momentarily on one sagging stone. Then she plummeted after him.

She landed on something that felt like a big, furry cushion. It was Ludo.

Hoggle, having rolled down Ludo's back, was now trapped beneath his great bulk, bellowing in terror.

Sarah gasped. "Ludo!"

Ludo put his head back, and howled.

"S-M-M-E-L-L-L-L-L-L!"

He was crouched on a little shoal beside the bog, which had been imperceptible from the height of the ledge. From only a few feet away, the stench of the putrid morass was cubed in intensity.

Sarah put her hands over her face. "Oooh! Aaarghh!"

Hoggle was struggling to get from under Ludo. "Help!" he shouted, in spite of the intake of foul air that shouting entailed. "Let me out!"

Sarah could not see where Hoggle was trapped. She assumed he was just frightened. She reassured him. "It's all right, Hoggle. He's a friend, too. This is Ludo."

"S-M-M-E-L-L-L-L-L-L!" Ludo wailed.

Sarah found that it helped if she pinched her nose tightly and used only the corner of her mouth to breathe and speak. "You can put me down now, Ludo," she said gratefully.

He complied, with a gentle care remarkable in so large a body.

Then Sarah saw Hoggle's plight. "Ludo," she said. "Let him get up. It's Hoggle."

Crawling out, Hoggle at once resumed his testy tone. "What do you mean, he's your friend? *I'm* your friend."

"You're *both* my friends," Sarah said. "I need you."

"Not as much as I need me," Hoggle answered, shuddering at the lake of muck.

"You're impossible," Sarah muttered from the side of her mouth.

"No, I'm not. I'm just as possible as you are. More possible, if the truth be told."

Sarah shrugged. She turned to Ludo, wanting to know how he had reached here from the forest of bones. But Ludo had been using his eyes while the other two were bickering, and now he pointed.

They looked, and saw a rustic bridge. It ran from a point farther along the shoal they were standing on, across a narrow neck of the bog, where a few sick-looking trees grew out of the mire, and finished on the opposite shore. Beyond it stretched a forest.

More forest. Sarah shook her head resignedly. Well, whatever perils or paradoxes that forest might hold, it offered more chance of traveling on to the castle than they had on this side, with the vast cliff and the Great Goblin Wall behind them, and the bog a few yards in front of them, bubbling and fermenting. "Come on," she said, and led the way. "Let's get across quickly."

The three of them picked their way along the narrow shoal. The stones and pebbles were loose beneath their feet, and an incautious step could skid them into the loathsome mire.

With Sarah in the lead, they approached the bridge. The sticks of wood of which it was constructed were pretty much the same color as the bog, as though they had been impregnated by it. The very air seemed tinted and heavy with the odor.

The bridge stood on piers of stone. They were only a few steps away from the nearest pier when a belligerent little figure came running out from behind it and confronted them.

"Stop!" he said, with an air of authority, as though there were nothing more that needed to be said.

He was courtly in appearance, wearing a smart jerkin, cut in the military style, and a cap with a plume in it. His mustache was white and aristocratically long, and his legs, though thin, were held still and apart. A bushy tail rose proudly from beneath his jerkin. His right hand held a staff. Altogether he gave the impression of a character who, though diminutive, was used to commanding and to being obeyed.

Sarah, by now reduced to pinching her nose and holding the sleeve of her shirt over her mouth to keep out the pervasive stench, mumbled, "Oh, please! We've got to get over—"

"Without my permission no one may cross."

"Who are you?" Sarah asked.

He bowed briskly from the waist. "Sir Didymus is my name, milady."

"Please, Sir Didymus," Sarah besought him. "I've only got a little more time left."

Hoggle nodded in eager agreement. "We got to get out of the stench."

"Smmelllll," Ludo moaned, frowning so expressively that his eyes disappeared beneath his brow and the corners of his mouth reached the edges of his jawbone.

"Stench?" Sir Didymus inquired. "Of what speakest thou?"

"The smell!" Sarah removed a hand from her mouth to point at the air.

Sir Didymus took several keen sniffs, sampled them in his nostrils, and shook his head, puzzled. "I smell nothing."

"You're joking," Hoggle told him.

Politely, Sir Didymus applied himself to understanding their problem. Holding himself erect, he ventilated his nostrils with several cubic feet of air. He shook his head again. "I live by my sense of smell. Yet I detect nothing."

The others, nauseated and dumbfounded, stared at him while he continued to inhale deeply. "The air," he pronounced, "is sweet and fragrant." Gripping his staff he added, "And none may pass without my permission."

Ludo threw back his head, and howled.

"S-M-M-E-L-L-L-L B-A-A-D!"

Hoggle barked, "Get out of the way!" and attempted to rush past and over the bridge.

Sir Didymus raised his staff and stood in the way. "I warn thee. I am sworn to do my duty."

Hoggle was desperate. He put his head down and charged. But Sir Didymus, moving agilely on his feet, arrested him with the point of his staff held intimidatingly at Hoggle's breast.

Ludo, bemused by the whole affair, was galvanized into activity when he saw one whom Sarah called "friend" being threatened. He advanced his great body toward Sir Didymus, pointed at Hoggle, and in a voice of reproach declared, "Friend."

"Then have at thee, too." With reckless gallantry, Sir Didymus launched himself at Ludo, flashing his staff in a dazzling series of thrusts. Ludo was forced to retreat.

Hoggle took the opportunity to dive around behind Sir Didymus, and make a run for the bridge, but the dauntless defender of the true faith was ready for him. In a bound he was back in position, his staff leveled at Hoggle.

While Hoggle screeched to a halt, then took several careful steps away again, Sir Didymus was flaring his proud nostrils and taking deep breaths. He appreciated the fresh air, but most of all he was enjoying the exercise. Not many travelers passed that way, and fewer still were prepared to test his knightly skills by trying to force their way over the bridge. In fact, no one had ever tried it before.

Sir Didymus had practiced his staffplay, ready for this moment. Now that it had arrived, it was a delicious treat. His blood thrilled and his sinews stiffened as he enacted the chivalric code of courage against all odds. This was the life. This was what he had been born for and sworn most solemnly to uphold. He would gladly have fought off a hundred Hoggles and a thousand Ludos, had such an army come tramping along and ventured the crossing of his bridge. He wished devoutly that such a horde would come, properly armed for the combat. How might a knight prove his valor, except it be tested?

Sarah walked forward. In a reasonable tone of voice, she pleaded, "Oh, look, let us cross your bridge, won't you?"

Sir Didymus answered her with his staff, lunging forward with one knee bent and brandishing the stick several times in front of her, using his wrist dexterously. Sarah recoiled.

That was more than Ludo could stand to see. With a great roar of anger he set about Sir Didymus. The tiny knight responded vigorously, with lunge and thrust. Deft footwork danced him out of reach of Ludo's massive swipes. Sir Didymus made adroit use of the terrain, skipping on and off the parapet of the pier, tripping nimbly along the very brink of the bog. As for Ludo, he had no finesse, but his ire and the strength of his bulk kept him shuffling after his adversary, ignoring the bruises that were inflicted upon him. Had just one of Ludo's blows landed, it would have been enough to knock Sir Didymus clean over the bog.

While the fight went on and on, Hoggle craftily seized his opportunity to scuttle across the bridge. Sarah watched him with dismay. He was just looking after himself again. There was little that he, or she, could do to assist, but she felt strongly that they owed Ludo their moral support.

Bits of the bridge fell off as Hoggle pounded over it. The whole structure shook and rattled.

At least Hoggle had the decency to stop, when he reached the far bank, and watch the rest of the epic battle. Sarah had expected him to vanish into the forest. Perhaps she was winning the battle with Hoggle's thick skin. Gradually, she was getting through to him.

The present battle was still locked. Holding her nose, Sarah cheered Ludo on, but there was no sign of victory for either side. Sir Didymus swung his staff, Ludo grabbed it and wrenched. Instead of being disarmed, Sir Didymus clung on, and was carried up in the air, legs kicking. Ludo lost hold of the twisting stick, and Sir Didymus thudded to the ground. He was up and at it again like a rubber ball, thwacking away at Ludo's shaggy legs.

Surprised by the minuscule martinet's ferocity, Ludo stood off for a moment, whereupon Sir Didymus took the opportunity to dive between his opponent's legs, crawl up his tail, as though storming a battlement, and belabor the back of Ludo's head. With a jerk of his neck, Ludo threw Sir Didymus clean over his head, then peered left and right for his plucky opponent, who was holding on to Ludo's whiskers and dangling beneath his chin. Ludo felt an itch and raised his hand to scratch it. He got Sir Didymus's teeth in his finger. With a howl, Ludo flicked his hand. Sir Didymus was shaken off and flew through the air until he hit the cliff. He was bouncing back in a trice, buzzing with the chance all this was giving him at last to prove his mettle.

Now Ludo had found a log and was crashing it down at Sir Didymus, but it was like trying to swat a fly with a club. All it did was make pits in the shoal. Sir Didymus took cover under the exposed roots of a mangy tree. Ludo advanced and brought the log down with such force that he smashed the roots and the tree keeled over.

For a moment, there was stillness. Ludo gaped. He had killed the little knight. He sighed, feeling wretched, till Sir Didymus darted out of a hole in the trunk of the tree.

Both of them were exhausted by now. Sir Didymus's legs were too tired to risk getting close enough to wound Ludo. Ludo could not swipe fast enough to hit Sir Didymus.

Eventually it was the diminutive chevalier who leaped back into his position on the bridge, raised his staff, *sans peur et sans reproche*, and gasped, "Enough! Thou fightest as a true and valiant knight."

Ludo gratefully accepted the truce. He sat down on his haunches, panting, and when he had recovered his breath he used it to bellow, "S-M-M-E-L-L-L!"

Sir Didymus regarded him with admiration. "Before this day," quoth he, "never have I met my match in combat." He smiled ruefully at Sarah. "Yet this noble knight has fought me to a standstill, quite."

Sarah's concern was all for Ludo. "Are you all right?" she asked him tenderly. "Ludo?"

Ludo was still recovering. "Uhhh..."

Sir Didymus marched, wearily but still smartly, to confront his equal in combat. "Sir Ludo, if that be thy name," he declared. "Here I yield my staff to thee." He held it out before him.

Ludo glanced at the staff without much interest. He was preparing to utter yet another howl about the stench, in the hope that someone could do something about it. He opened his mouth.

Sir Didymus continued his speech. "Let us be brothers henceforth, and fight for the right as one."

Ludo's mouth remained open, but he postponed the howl. His face, beaming, came down to regard Sir Didymus. "Ludo—get—brother?"

The pocket-sized pursuivant, bushy tail erect, went to clap his brother-in-arms on the shoulder, which he could just reach since Ludo was almost prone. "Well met, Sir Ludo."

"Ludo—sir?"

Sarah thought she would soon die if she had to go on breathing in this fetid air. She was trying not to breathe at all. Seeing that the two noble knights had apparently reached a satisfactory agreement, she said, "Good. Come on, then."

She made for the bridge, but Sir Didymus was there before her, blocking the way. "Hold!" he cried. "You forget my sacred vow, milady. I cannot let you pass."

It wasn't possible. Sarah thought she might pick the little figure up and hurl him far into the bog. But he had raised his staff again and was holding it toward her. "Oh..." She made a noise of frustration through her pinched nose. "You said Ludo was your brother. Surely in that case..."

Sir Didymus replied with a firm shake of his head. "I have taken an oath. I must defend it to the death."

"SMELL!" Ludo bayed.

Sarah closed her eyes and gave it some thought. "Okay," she said, "let's handle this thing logically. What exactly have you sworn?"

Sir Didymus raised his staff high above his head and gazed up at it devoutly. "With my lifeblood have I sworn, that none shall pass this way without my permission."

Sarah nodded. "Ah," she said, and considered the point. "Then," she asked slowly, "may we have your permission?"

Complete silence followed her question. Sir Didymus was thunderstruck. He tried looking at the proposition from one side, then from the other. He turned it upside down and inside out. He went away from it and came back to take a fresh look at it. No matter how he tried it, he could see no flaw in what Sarah had suggested. Finally, he shrugged, drew himself up straight, looked from Sarah's face to Ludo's and back again, and delivered his considered conclusion. "Yes."

"Good," Sarah said, trying not to breathe deeply with the relief. "Shall we go?" She gestured past Sir Didymus to the bridge. At the far side of it she could see Hoggle still waiting.

Sir Didymus executed a gallant bow, and offered her the bridge with a flourish of his hand. "Milady."

"Well, thank you, noble sir," Sarah said, and stepped onto the rickety bridge.

CHAPTER XIII
ONCE BITTEN

The moment Sarah's foot landed on the bridge, the whole structure creaked and settled down a couple of inches. She jumped off again quickly.

"Have no fear, sweet madam," Sir Didymus reassured her. "This bridge has stood a thousand years."

Sarah looked warily at the bridge. "I just hope it stands another five minutes." She put her foot on it again and felt it sway beneath her. Gingerly, with a hand held out for Ludo to grab if need be, she put her whole weight on the bridge. It settled again, with a noise like a very dry hinge. A couple of fragments fell off, with a puff of dust, and plopped into the bubbling bog.

One hand on the rickety handrail, the other arm outstretched like a tightrope walker, Sarah advanced a step, then another. There were noises of squeaking and cracking at every movement she made. Behind her she heard a dull splash. A stone in the pier, loosened by her weight, had fallen. She felt the plank beneath her feet give another inch. The only thing that made her go on was the certainty that she had no alternative.

Sir Didymus, in contrast, had no qualms. He was giving no more thought to the bridge, in fact. His brain was glowing with the prospect of, at last, submitting himself to the supreme test of the chivalric code—a quest. He had no idea what these people's purpose was, but it was clear that they must have one, from the sense of urgency that his trained eye had detected in the damsel. It was, moreover, a purpose of such high import that her courtiers were willing to engage in unarmed combat with a warrior such as himself in order to achieve it. His skin tingled and his eyes flashed as he turned to Ludo, and said, "Since thou art my brother, I will come with thee whate'er thy quest. Lead on!" With a little bow and a flourish of his hand, he invited Ludo to follow Sarah across the bridge.

Ludo shook his head. "Ludo—wait!"

And even as Ludo eyed the bridge suspiciously, another large chunk of masonry crumbled out of the pier and rolled into the bog. The bridge suddenly sagged and swayed. Sarah grabbed hold of the handrail with both hands. Other stones and loose cement were falling from the pier. In the middle of the shaking, sinking bridge, Sarah was stranded. She looked around in horror, saw that the whole thing was collapsing, and made a run for it to the other side.

Too late. With a screeching, rending noise, the rotten timbers gave way beneath her. The vile muck bubbled over the edges of the planks in front of her. Sarah leaped for the overhanging branch of an ailing, leafless tree beside the bridge and managed to get both hands onto it. Swinging there, looking down at the crust of scum bubbling beneath her feet, and at the remains of the bridge floating on the bog, she moaned at the thought of being stained and stinking forever. With each swing she heard the branch tearing away from its trunk. "Help!" she cried pitifully. "Ludo! Hoggle! Sir Didymus! Help! Do something!"

Sir Didymus was transfixed. His bridge had been erased from the landscape. It took him a little time to accustom himself to the new view, and a little more to accept that the role he had always played so devoutly had now been abolished. Then he remembered that he had just dedicated himself to these people's quest.

"Fear not, fair maiden," he called out to Sarah. "I will rescue thee." He looked around giddily for the means. "Somehow," he called encouragingly.

Sarah, feet swinging, hearing the branch splitting, gurgled, "Help!"

Sir Didymus held his staff out toward Sarah. It bridged about a thirtieth of the gap between them. "Here!" he shouted.

Hoggle, on the far bank, just closed his eyes.

Ludo sat back on his haunches, threw back his head, opened his huge mouth and howled ten times more loudly than he had when the goblins had been tormenting him.

Sir Didymus gaped round at the amazing noise. "By the saints in their stockings!" he exclaimed. "Can I believe my ears?"

Sarah felt the branch starting to lower her and screamed, but none of the others could hear her above Ludo's earth-shaking roar.

Sir Didymus was shocked. "Sir Ludo, my brother!" he said reproachfully. "Art thou the manly knight I fought e'en now? Canst thou sit by and do no more than howl when yon damsel stands in need of our most gallant assistance?"

"HOOOOOWWWWWLL!" Ludo continued.

Sarah's feet were by now wriggling only inches above the khaki-colored slime. She bent her knees up to postpone the dreadful moment of contact, but she could feel that the branch was tearing its last fibers.

From the far side of the bog, a rumbling noise could be heard, growing louder as it approached. A huge rock was rolling itself across the ground. Hoggle, hearing the noise behind him, had to jump out of the way. The boulder went past him, slipped itself gently into the bog, and came to rest, breaking the surface, immediately underneath Sarah's feet. As it arrived there, the branch cracked off the tree. Sarah landed on the dry rock, curled up and crumpled. She lay there sobbing with relief, but nearly asphyxiated by the stench a few inches from her nose.

Ludo's howling had not been a cry of useless dismay. The stones of the earth had saved him not long since, when Sarah's aim at the tormenting goblins' helmets had proved so accurate. Now he was summoning them again.

Sir Didymus was openmouthed. He kept turning his head, looking from the boulder to Ludo and back again, unable to decide which element of the miracle more deserved his attention, cause or effect, brother or rock.

Ludo was not done. His head was still back, and he sustained his howling. This time he was answered by rocks dwelling beneath the mire. One by one they came to the surface, shedding the slime as though it were egg white. They stood themselves side by side, until they had created a perfectly flat causeway stretching from Sarah's rock to each side of the bog.

Sarah stood up. She gazed at Ludo and shook her head in wonder. Then she smiled, gratefully blew him a kiss, and ran across the causeway to the far shore, where Hoggle held out his hand to help her onto the dry ground.

"Oh!" Sir Didymus sighed in a low, respectful voice, and looked ardently at this most potent knight, the flower of chivalry, his brother. In almost a whisper, he asked, "Canst thou then summon up the very rocks, Sir Ludo?"

"Rocks—friends." Ludo stood up, and charged joyfully across his causeway to rejoin Sarah.

"Sir Ludo!" Sir Didymus called after him. "Wait for me." He did not want to lose this noble company. He looked around and barked out. "Ambrosius! My noble steed!"

From behind a tree, a wooly Old English sheepdog poked his nose warily out. When he saw that it was safe, he trotted obediently up to his master, panting in anticipation.

Sarah, waiting on the far side of the bog, was incredulous when she saw Ambrosius. He was the identical twin of Merlin (who, she thought glumly, was probably still confined to the garage). "That's your steed?" she called to Sir Didymus.

"Indeed it is," Sir Didymus called back, mounting up. "And no knight has one better—fleet and surefooted in battle, loyal and obedient in peaceful times, he is a flawless mount. Except when he sees a cat." He squeezed Ambrosius in the ribs with his heels. "Onward," he commanded.

Ambrosius carried him at a trot over the causeway. There, Sir Didymus dismounted and led his steed, walking beside Sarah and Ludo. The valiant knight was agog to hear how perilous their quest was to be, but he contained his impatience like the perfect gentleman that he was.

Sarah looked around for Hoggle. The dwarf was still hanging around the edge of the bog. Could he have gotten to *like* it there? "Come on, Hoggle," Sarah called.

Hoggle was vacillating in a hogglish dilemma. His hand was in the pouch that hung from his belt, fingering the peach. If he gave it to Sarah, he would be betraying his heart. If he did not give it to her, he would be dumped headfirst in the Bog of Stench.

He brought the peach out and held it over the bog. He had not quite reached his decision yet, but he reckoned it would be wise to be prepared to act instantly once he had, with no time to change his mind. The peach might even slip accidentally from his fingers and relieve him of the responsibility of making the choice.

He was still holding the peach over the fetid scum when he heard a voice in the air above his head. "I wouldn't do that if I were you," it said.

Hoggle was so startled that he almost dropped the peach. But his fingers tightened around it. He closed his eyes in anguish. Jareth, wherever he was, was watching him. "Please," Hoggle whispered, "I can't give it to her."

He felt his feet sliding toward the brink of the bog.

"No!" Hoggle squealed. "No! All *right!*"

He put the peach back in the pouch and walked miserably toward the others.

Sir Didymus had been fretting at the delay. When he saw that Hoggle was following at last, he decided that the expedition needed brisker leadership. He was the one to do it, as long as they would tell him where they wanted him to lead them. He mounted Ambrosius again and headed into the forest, since it was obvious that they all had some unfathomable aversion to the bog. Ludo and Sarah followed him. Hoggle trailed some way behind.

For a while, they went along in silence. Sir Didymus frowned and sucked his teeth, reflecting on the travails and perils through which he and Sir Ludo, his legendary brother, would be expected to lead the company. But withal, he thought, spurring on Ambrosius, thus is it and must always be in the knightly vocation. Be thou afraid or easily deterred, then let thee never bow thy knee to receive the sword of honor upon thy craven shoulder.

Ludo, walking behind Sir Didymus, was thinking how good it was to breathe sweet air again, and how hungry he was.

Sarah shared those thoughts, but mostly she was preoccupied with how Toby was faring, and with how much time might remain of the thirteen hours Jareth had given her.

Hoggle was thinking of the choice he had not made, and of what, in consequence, he now had to do to Sarah. If she knew, he thought, she could scarcely blame me, could she? How would *she* like to be suspended *headfirst* in the Bog? No, it's all Jareth's fault. I'm just obeying an order that I can't refuse.

Sarah realized that she had no idea where Sir Didymus was leading them. She asked him.

"Whithersoever thy quest demandeth," he answered. He had never felt so happy.

"Do you know the way to the castle?"

"To anysoever castle thou namest, fair and gentle damsel. The Castle of Perseverance? The Castle of Tintagel? The Castle—"

"Jareth's castle."

"Ah. In Goblin City." Sir Didymus nodded. He had been hoping for a quest that would take seven years to perform, but he did not show his disappointment. Perhaps this was a trial, and something more enduring would come of it. "Ambrosius knows these woods well," he said. "We shall reach the town well before day doth break tomorrow." He gave Ambrosius's reins a brisk shake and trotted purposefully ahead.

Tomorrow, Sarah was thinking anxiously. Tomorrow will be too late to save Toby, assuming that the sun takes twenty-four hours, or maybe twenty-six, to cycle around here. She looked at the sky, through the forest branches, and saw that it was evening. Pink and amber ribbons of cloud were lit by the declining sun. "How many hours will that be?" she asked.

Sir Didymus shrugged. "I know not hours, sweet maiden. A knight must perforce reckon his life by intervals of seven years."

"Oh." Sarah looked at Ludo, but knew that he would know nothing about clocks.

Ludo caught her glance. "Hungry," he said sadly.

"We can't stop," Sarah told him, "but maybe there are some berries or something."

She looked for Hoggle. Perhaps he might have some idea of the time.

Hoggle saw her looking back for him, and waiting for him to catch up, and he knew that the time had come. He forced himself to alter his demeanor, switched on a glassy smile, drove his feet into a perky stride, and came swaggering up, good old Hoggle, trusty friend. "Missy," he said, beaming, and held out his hand.

In it Sarah saw the most luscious peach, so rich and ripe and tantalizingly juicy that it appeared to be glowing. She realized that Ludo was not the only one who was hungry. Oh, kind Hoggle! He must have heard them talking about food.

She held her hand out toward the peach. It looked so large and delicious that they could each have a mouthful of it. "Hoggle," she said gratefully, "you're a lifesaver."

She wondered if she should politely offer the others first bite, but by now it was in her hand, and Hoggle was looking so pleased to have given it to her that she felt it was expected of her to take a bite. She raised it to her lips, then held it away again to look at it. The scent was beautiful.

Hoggle, fists clenching, glanced up at Ludo and Sir Didymus and saw that they had not stopped, but were a distance away. That was something.

Sarah looked at the peach almost with regret. It was a pity to spoil such a lovely thing. Although that was the point, wasn't it? A peach made itself lovely just so that someone would spoil it. But if that were the case, it was clever to be repulsive, and rattlesnakes might rule the earth one day. Was that what they had in mind?

She bit into the peach.

The sound of her biting made Hoggle tremble. He wanted to put his hands over his ears.

Sarah's face was rapt. "This tastes… so strange." She looked at the peach, and found that her eyes would not focus on it. She began to sway. Feeling that she might be going to faint, she took a step toward Hoggle, for support. She stumbled. With one hand she wiped her brow while, with the other, she held the peach out at arm's length, trying to look at it properly. Then she understood. Slowly, she looked at Hoggle. He was a blurred, shimmering shape. "Hoggle," she said quietly. "What have you done?"

In a strangled voice, Hoggle cried out, "Damn you, Jareth! And damn me, too!" Turning his face away from Sarah, he ran headlong into the forest.

Now Sarah was tottering. She managed to stagger to a tree, and leaned against it. She had already forgotten Hoggle and Ludo and Sir Didymus and Toby, and where she was and why. All her thoughts were for Jareth, and her eyes were looking up at the sky.

"Everything's dancing," she whispered.

CHAPTER XIV
O BODY SWAYED TO MUSIC

Jareth held four crystal balls close to his face. He stared into each of them in turn, catching the light. It seemed as though he were choosing among them. He took one of them and swirled it into the air, with a flick of his wrist. It floated away from him, became a bubble. Then it drifted through the open window beside which he was standing, and away through the darkening sky. The other three followed in turn, coldly beautiful bubbles floating through the dusk, turning and gleaming, mesmeric globes glowing in the dying light.

Sarah was still leaning limply against the tree, too dizzy to move, when the four bubbles approached her in the sky. She stared at them, entranced. She watched as the dazzling spheres floated toward her, slowly descending. They were dancing with the light, and she could hear music, an aching, haunting music, solemn, like a pavane. She was rapt. Her lips parted in wonder. The bubbles were close enough now for her to see that within the first of them was the dancer from her music box, twirling pirouettes. In each of the other three bubbles was another dancer, moving with sinuous elegance.

Sarah's body swayed hypnotically in time with the music. She was the music and the dance. She was inside a bubble, dancing, dressed in a ball gown. Enchanted and enchanting, she danced slowly across the sky in company with the other dancers.

A congregation of many bubbles crossed the night sky, each with a dancer within it. They were approaching one great bubble, as though attracted by some magnetic force. Inside the great bubble was a magnificent ballroom. Jareth was already dancing there.

Sir Didymus and Ludo had come to the edge of the forest, and now they looked out across the bare, dry, cracked plain to the distant walls of the castle.

Sir Didymus patted Ambrosius, who had found the way. "Good work, oh loyal steed," he told the dog. He half turned his head to call behind him, with a trace of smugness, "Yonder lies the castle, my lady."

He heard no answer and turned fully around to see where Sarah was. Ludo too turned around, a growl of suspicion in his throat. Together they stared back down the trail they had followed.

Sarah had vanished.

"My lady?" Sir Didymus was shouting. "My lady?"

Above their heads a bubble floated past, moving in the direction of the castle.

The ballroom had known opulence. Between glittering cornices were hung many long chandeliers where the wax, dripping for a hundred years, had formed stalactites. The silk covering of the walls had faded and, in places, worn threadbare. Bubbles decorated the room, and the whole of it was contained within the iridescent skin of one great bubble. A tall, gilt, thirteen-hour clock stood in a corner. It was almost twelve o'clock.

Sarah watched the dance, and the dancers watched her, from behind their masks. The men sported silken shirts open to the waist and tight velvet breeches. Some of them wore wide-brimmed, plumed hats; others had capes or carried staffs. The women's gowns left their shoulders bare and dove low between their breasts. They had their hair coiffed high, and many wore long gloves.

The dancers moved in a ring around the ballroom, with a kind of lethargic brilliance, as though the party had been going on all night. Men who were not dancing lounged indolently against the columns, or in a cushioned pit in the center of the ballroom, in the company of women. Maids and footmen, with skin the color of old parchment, served them trays of fruit and refilled their goblets from decanters. And always the dancers were watching through the eyeholes in their cruel half-masks, from which snouts projected and horns sprouted above. Moving together or elegantly reclined, they watched Sarah, or watched each other watching, and beneath the masks the mouths smiled at each other like knives.

Sarah's gown was silvery, the color of mother-of-pearl, with puffed short sleeves. She had a pearl necklace on, and her hair was braided with strings of pearls. Her eyes were wide. She was the picture of innocence in that setting, a picture that excited the dancers, who never took their masked eyes off her, while they moved with weary grace to the cadence of a sinisterly beautiful tune.

She walked slowly around the room. Two gorgeously gowned women snickered behind their fans at her. Sarah paused beside a tall mirror and looked at her image.

The people passing behind her, in the mirror, were watching her like ravishing birds of prey. The dancers swayed and swirled. Then

Sarah saw something in the mirror that made her gasp. She had caught a glimpse of Jareth, entwined with a voluptuous woman, dancing past.

She whirled around, but he had vanished. She stood there, peering through the throng for him so intently that she did not notice the young man leaning against the column beside her. He had his head held back and was staring brazenly at her. He relished her face, then her white shoulders, her breasts, hips, and legs, and moved closer to her. He murmured into her ear, "You are remarkably beautiful, my dear girl."

Sarah spun around to face him, her mouth open. At the mixture of surprise and pleasure on her face, the young man threw back his head and laughed. She smiled back at him nervously.

Hidden behind another man's cape, Jareth had watched it all, but Sarah had not seen him watching. His eyes were following Sarah wherever she went in the corrupt ballroom.

She was tense now, self-conscious, among people she could not understand but who behaved as though they knew something that she didn't know. She moved hurriedly around the ballroom looking for Jareth. She did not know why she wanted to find him, or what she would say to him. She just knew that it was vitally important that she *should* find him.

When she saw him, he was whispering something to his beautiful partner, who responded by smiling knowingly from beneath her mask and licking her lips, slowly, with the tip of her tongue.

Sarah blushed and turned away in embarrassment. She found herself looking into another of the tall mirrors around the room. Behind her she saw Jareth, standing alone. He was a resplendent figure, upright and blond, in a midnight blue frock coat, diamanté at the neck, shoulders, and cuffs. Ruffs of pale gray silk at his throat and wrists set off the pallor of his skin. On his legs he was wearing black tights and black, shiny boots. He was holding a horned mask on a stick, but he had lowered it now, to look straight at Sarah in the mirror. Behind him, dancers were whirling. He held his hand out.

She turned around, not expecting that he would really be there. He was, and he was still holding out his hand to her. She took it, feeling dizzy.

Her dizziness ceased when she went spinning around the ballroom in Jareth's arms. She was the loveliest woman at the ball. She knew it, from the way in which Jareth was smiling down at her. All his attention was on her. The touch of his hands on her body was thrilling. To dance with him seemed the easiest and most natural motion. When he told her that she was beautiful, she felt confused.

"I feel… I feel like… I—don't know what I feel."

He was amused. "Don't you?"

"I feel like… I'm in a dream, but I don't remember ever dreaming anything like this!"

He pulled back to look at her and laughed, but fondly. "You'll have to find your way into the part," he said, and whirled her on around the room.

She smiled up at him. She thought how handsome he was, but one didn't tell a man such things, did one? More than that, there was something in his face that was openly enjoying the moment, without the mocking or secretiveness that she had seen on other faces here.

"And when you've found your way in, stay in your dream, Sarah." Jareth's eyes were looking straight into hers. His smile was serious. "Believe me. If you want to be truly free, wholly yourself—you do want that, don't you?"

Sarah nodded.

"Then you will find what you want only as long as you stay in your dream. Once abandon it, and you are at the mercy of other people's dreams. They will make of you what *they* want you to be. Forget them, Sarah. Trust to your dream."

Sarah was spellbound.

"Trust to me," Jareth said, moving his face close to hers. "Can you do that?"

She nodded, and looked up at him with anticipation. He was going to kiss her. She shut her eyes. That was the way to do it.

Something made her open her eyes again. It was the silence. The music had stopped. She saw that they had been surrounded by all the other dancers. They were leering and nudging each other. She saw them biting their lips to hold back their laughter. Jareth seemed to be unperturbed, but she turned her face sharply away from his, horrified. He held her more tightly, and insistently sought her lips with his. Suffused with disgust, she wrenched herself free of him.

The clock struck twelve.

Sarah pushed her way through the jostling, jeering crowd. A man smiled foxily at her behind his mask and then grasped at her body. She smelled his evil breath on her face. She shoved him away angrily. A group of giggling women rushed between them, chased by merrily guffawing men. Sarah was knocked off balance and stumbled against a column. Crouching, frightened, she made her way out of the crowd, until she saw the shimmering membrane of the great bubble just in front of her.

Beside her was a small, painted chair. She picked it up in both hands, and hurled it at the bubble.

The chair crashed through it. As the bubble burst, Sarah was sucked through it.

She was flying through space. Below, on the ground, she saw the faces of Ludo and Sir Didymus looking up at her. Their mouths were moving, as if they were calling out to her, but all she could hear was the thrum of rushing air. Behind her, the ballroom had collapsed and crumbled to junk. Strange things, and pieces of things, and things of pieces, were whizzing through space with her, some overtaking her, some receding.

She started to recognize objects. The dancer from her music box pirouetted past, upside down, followed by several of her favorite books, in random order, their pages flapping loose in the wind. Launcelot was not far away in the sky, and beyond him Sarah saw some gossip cuttings, and the spoon and egg cup she had used when she was a baby. It was an aerial Sargasso Sea formed of everything she had ever seen or imagined but rearranged in improbable combinations. If this is the debris of the ballroom, she thought, then all my life must have been at that ball, in disguise.

The floating junk room of her mind stretched from horizon to horizon. It was all speeding up, and beginning to spin around, faster and faster, in a maelstrom, Sarah with it. The rush of air became a screeching, untuned music.

It stopped. Sarah was on the ground, in her own clothes again. In her hand was the half-eaten peach. She held it up to examine it more closely. Its flesh was rotten. A maggot crept out from the pit. Sarah gasped, and flung the peach away, and fainted.

CHAPTER XV
THE TIME OF HER LIFE

Sarah woke up in nowhere. She opened her eyes and above her saw a somber sky, but the bare ground beside her was harshly lit, like pictures she had seen of the moon. Perhaps she *was* on the moon, for all she knew.

She had been at a ball, that much she could remember. Where it was, and how she had gotten there, and why—nothing came back to her; just the ball. She closed her eyes at the memory of Jareth, hot with shame at how she had succumbed to his charm. She felt soiled by what had ensued in the ballroom. Somehow, it had all been her fault. Those men who pawed her, Jareth trying so rudely to force a kiss upon her—had she been truly innocent, they would not have behaved like that toward her, would they?

"What was I doing?" she asked aloud. She sat up and looked about her. What she saw was an utterly desolate landscape, a desert whose only features were heaps and scraps of junk. Sarah's face was blank with despair. There was nothing to do here, nothing. No one in sight. It was a place where you would soon forget your own name.

With an effort, she stood up. The first step she took landed on a small pile of rags. The rags moved, suddenly, beneath her foot. She jumped back.

" 'Ere!" said an old woman's voice. "Git orf my back!"

"Sorry," Sarah apologized instinctively, without knowing whom or what she was addressing.

A section of the rags rose up. Sarah saw that it was actually a pile of junk, stacked up on the bent back of a little old goblin woman. At the same time it dawned on her that other mounds of garbage were in reality (if anything here was reality) loads on the backs of other people, who were moving very slowly across the moonscape. She spotted the painted chair from the ballroom not far away, surmounting a pile that someone had collected.

The junk woman's puckered face was staring crossly at her from beneath the load of bent and battered metal objects, discarded clothes, chipped crockery, and broken furniture that she bore. "Why don't you look where you're going, young woman?"

"I *was* looking," Sarah answered, slightly aggrieved.

"Then where are you going?"

"Oh… er… well, I can't remember."

The junk woman sniffed. "You can't *look* where you're going if you don't *know* where you're going."

Sarah thought that they could have argued the point, but she decided politeness would serve her better. She looked around and said, "I mean, I was searching for something."

The junk woman chuckled, mollified. "Well, of course you was, dearie. We'se all searching for something, ain't we? But yer got to have sharp eyes if yer going to find anything. Now *me*, I found lots of thing." And she glanced upward, indicating the burden of junk piled up on her back.

Sarah looked harder at the woman's rubbish trove and found it curiously interested her. "Why," she exclaimed, "so you have!"

The junk woman grunted with satisfaction.

"There's a cookie tin," Sarah observed, "and a colander, and some pieces of candle…"

"Oh, yes." The junk woman was nodding. "It's hard to find classy stuff like this nowadays."

"I suppose so." Sarah was looking past the old woman. Occasionally a pile of junk would arise on the back of someone who wandered across to try the pickings in another mound. All of them were heading, desultorily, in the same direction, as though making for home at the end of the day.

"But don't you worry, dearie." The junk woman had become like a grandmother to her now. "I'll give you a few things, to get you started, like. How's that?"

"Oh," Sarah said uncertainly, "thank you."

The junk woman had started to trudge along in the same direction as the others. Sarah walked along beside her. As she went, the old woman rummaged with one hand among the pile of junk on her back, feeling for something. Sarah watched her anxiously, fearing that the whole load could come crashing down around her feet if she pulled out one item. Eventually the junk woman said, "Ha," and extracted what she wanted. She handed it to Sarah.

It was Launcelot.

Sarah swallowed, and smiled with childish joy. "Launcelot!" she cried, hugging him. "Thank you," she told the junk woman, "Thank you." It was as though she were again the little girl being given the teddy bear by her father.

"That's what you was looking for, ain't it?" the old woman asked, kindly.

Sarah nodded eagerly, clasping Launcelot. "Yes. I'd forgotten." She sighed, and gave the teddy bear a kiss.

"Now," the junk woman said, "why don't you go in there and see if there's anything else you'd like?" She was pointing to a sort of tent they had come to, as colorless as the rest of nowhere. The woman bent down and pulled back a flap of the tent.

Sarah took a step forward, saw what was inside the tent, and opened her eyes and mouth wide. It was her own room.

Sarah was lying on her bed at home, clasping her teddy bear. It was nighttime. She was still dressed.

She sat upright slowly, and looked around the room. Everything was where it should be. She rubbed her forehead. "Oh, it *was* just a dream." She looked at the teddy bear. "I dreamed it all, Launcelot." She shook her head, wonderingly. "It was so—so real, and so…" She gave Launcelot a squeeze. "I'm still a bit nervous."

She tiptoed across to the door of the room, still holding Launcelot. "I wonder if Daddy's back?" she whispered. Cautiously, in case they were asleep, she opened the door.

The junk woman was standing outside, peering concernedly at her. "Don't you like them fings, dearie?" Behind the old woman, the bleak, harshly lit moonscape stretched away.

Sarah slammed the door shut in the woman's face. She ran across to her bed and buried her head in the sheets. After a while she looked at Launcelot and said firmly, "It is a dream." She closed her eyes, and forced herself to breathe calmly. "It's a dream," she said, and nodded. She held Launcelot tight. "It is a *dream*."

She stood up, taking a deep breath, and walked confidently to the door.

When she opened it, she saw the junk woman still waiting there. This time, she was in the room before Sarah could shut the door again. "Best to stay in here, dearie," the junk woman told her comfortingly. "There's nuffink you want out there." The woman gave Sarah a wink and a confidential smile.

Sarah had remained quite still, beside the door. "Launcelot," she whispered.

The junk woman was bustling around Sarah's room, picking things from the shelves and examining them, as though she were clearing out a house. But when she found something that caught her fancy, instead of adding it to her own pile she placed it in Sarah's arms. "Look, here's your nice fluffy rabbit. You likes your rabbit, don't you? And Raggedy Ann!" The woman smiled fondly. "You remember Raggedy Ann."

Sarah was distractedly following the woman along the line of shelves. That the woman could know and name these familiar possessions of hers was bewildering. Below the bewilderment, something else was working at Sarah's feelings, something gray and listless, like despair. She recognized it, but could not be sure of its cause.

What was it, this low feeling? It had to do, she suspected, with the way this old woman was fussing over her.

The junk woman was heaping more and more things into Sarah's arms. "And here's your shoe box—lots of pencils and elastic bands— you want all those. Oh, and look! Here's your panda slippers. You know how you loves your panda slippers... never wanted them to get thrown away."

Sarah sank down onto the chair in front of her dressing-table mirror. She spread all the objects in her arms upon the table and stared at herself.

"Ooh, and here's a treasure! You wants that, don't you, dearie?" The woman handed Sarah her broken lipstick. "Go on. Put it on."

Sarah took the lipstick from her and obediently started to apply it.

Meanwhile, the junk woman began to load ever more objects upon Sarah's back. Peculiarly, they stuck there, one on top of the other. Perhaps it was some trick of the trade.

"And here's your old horsie. You likes your horsie. *Horsie, horsie, don't you stop, just let your feet go clippety-clop.* Heh-heh. And all the Badger books... Oh, and here's dear old Flopsy. And the printing game. And your toy shop—it's still got the little candies in jars. And *The Wizard of Oz*. And there's the first knitting you ever done, just look. You want that, don't you, dearie?"

In the mirror, Sarah saw that the pile of stuff on her back was getting to be almost as tall a burden as the old junk woman herself bore. Moreover, her shoulders had started to look bowed. As if mesmerized, she stared into the mirror, into her own eyes, and in a distant voice said, "There was something I was looking for…"

"Don't talk rot," answered the old woman. "It's all here, everything you've ever cared about."

Sarah looked around at the junk woman, who was still happily poking among the shelves. She turned back to the mirror and went on applying the broken lipstick.

"And here's your ducky book," the woman was chanting. "You haven't forgotten how it goes up and down and quacks…"

Sarah stopped listening. She had to, or she would have wept with humiliation. She looked around for something to take her mind off the junk woman's condescending litany. On the far side of the dressing table was *The Labyrinth*, where she had left it. She put down the lipstick, opened the book and began to read aloud. "Through dangers untold and hardships unnumbered," she recited, "I have fought my way here to the castle beyond the Goblin City, to take back the child you have stolen…"

She laid the book in her lap and looked around the room. The old junk woman was still prattling on, but suddenly Sarah had risen above it. "The child you have stolen…" She remembered what it was she had been looking for. Toby!

Everything altered. The room was the same as it had always been, night and morning, day after day for as long as Sarah could remember, but she was seeing it with new eyes. It was all fabricated from pieces of scrap, everything was rubbish, relics. All her things, the furniture, even the walls, the whole room was a garbage heap, a dead shrine to a spirit that had fled.

The junk woman had noticed the new expression on Sarah's face and was asking her, in a concerned voice, "What's the matter, dearie? Don't you like your toys?"

"It's all junk."

The woman was taken aback. She stuck out her lower lip and made a grumbling noise to herself, as she shuffled around the room, looking for something, poking in drawers and along shelves. Eventually she found it and held it up decisively. "What about this?" she demanded. "This isn't junk."

It was her trump card, the music box. She gave Sarah a knowing look and turned the key. "Greensleeves" tinkled through the room, sounding strangely like the haunting music of the ballroom.

"Yes, it is!" It was junk like everything else there, the litter of a time of her life that she now passionately wanted to leave behind. She knew what the gray despair had been. This room was a prison, and she was her own jailer. And so she had the key to release herself, to go and do the thing that mattered.

"I've got to save Toby!" she cried.

Faintly, from somewhere beyond the room, she could hear her name being called. "Sarah, Sarah!" She recognized the voices. It was Ludo and Sir Didymus calling to her.

She stood up, hurling from her shoulders all the stuff the old junk woman had been sticking on her. At the same time, the walls of the room started to vibrate. Things tumbled down from shelves, handles rattled. Then the very walls began to fall apart, as though it were all jerry-built junk.

Sarah looked around to see what was happening. Through the crumbling ceiling, two pairs of hands appeared, reaching down. She seized hold of them, and the hands at once hauled her up, out of the room.

She rose from a pile of junk and was set down on the firm ground. Ludo was smiling; Sir Didymus looked brisk and courteous. "Fair maid," he said. "At last thou art with us again."

Behind them, she could see a great pair of grotesque gates. Beyond the gates was Jareth's castle.

CHAPTER XVI
THE GATES OF GOBLIN CITY

Sarah looked at the grotesque gates and did not dare to believe what she saw. "Where are we?" she asked.

All Ludo could do was beam with joy. "Sarah—back," he started to say.

Sir Didymus interrupted him. "We are at the gates of the Goblin City, fair damsel. Beyond thou canst descry the castle, the object of thy quest, didst thou not say?"

"That's right."

Sir Didymus looked wistful. "Thou art sure, art thou not, that thou dost not seek a castle that requireth fourteen years of knight errantry through travails and perils and—"

"O, Sir Didymus. Ludo. I have to go quickly into Jareth's castle, or I'll lose Toby."

"Toby?" Sir Didymus queried.

"My little brother."

"Toby—Ludo—brother," Ludo beamed.

"Ah! Sir Tobias, our brother-in-arms," Sir Didymus exclaimed.

"Then forward!" He raised his staff, spurred Ambrosius and charged toward the gates of Goblin City.

Sarah and Ludo hurried after him. They did not see a shadowy figure lurking behind a junk pile. It was Hoggle, and he was watching every move they made.

Outside the gates, a goblin guard was leaning on his spear, sound asleep. Sir Didymus took no notice of him, but rushed straight at the great gates and began to hammer on them with his staff. "Open up!" he bellowed. "Open the gates, in the name of all that is—"

Sarah, catching up with him, put her finger anxiously on her lips and whispered, "Sh! Quiet, Sir Didymus." She pointed to the sleeping guard.

Sir Didymus glanced contemptuously, and shouted, "Pshaw! I give not a fig for such goblins." He repeated his clattering on the gates. "Open up, I say!"

"*Please*," Sarah entreated him in an urgent whisper. She saw the guard grunt and stir in his deep sleep.

Sir Didymus was indomitable. "Let them all wake up. I shall fight them to the death." And again he rained blows upon the resounding gates.

The guard's eyelids were flickering.

Sarah grabbed the tiny chevalier by the sleeve. "*Please! Please*, Sir Didymus. For my sake, could you please try to make no noise?"

From his saddle, Sir Didymus bowed so low that his mustache swept the ground. "But of course," he assured her. "For thee, fairest of maidens, for thee, anything!" He put his mouth to her ear, and whispered, "But I am not a coward?"

"Oh, no," she whispered back.

Ludo shook his head, too, with great conviction.

Sir Didymus had one more point concerning his knightly prowess that he wished to settle. "And my sense of smell is keen?"

"Oh, yes," Sarah told him.

Sir Didymus drew himself up proudly, and his voice rose again. "Then will I fight anybody or anyone, at any time, anywhere." He thought, and shouted, "With any weapons."

Sarah was pressing her finger to her lips again. "We know, we know," she whispered. "Now please, Sir Didymus, shusheth thee up."

"Right," he said with alacrity.

Meanwhile, Ludo had gone up to the gates and given one of them a little push. It swung open.

The three of them sneaked inside. As soon as they had done so, they heard the gates slam shut behind them. Ahead of them was another pair of gates. This pair was already open.

"Ah!" Sir Didymus exclaimed, with a proud toss of his head. "They dare not shut their gates against the might of Sir Didymus." And, holding his staff aloft, the flower of chivalry led his intrepid band onward.

The inner pair of gates, however, swung shut before Sir Didymus reached them. And the appearance they now presented was a thousand times more daunting than mere gates. Each door was half a giant suit of armor. When the two halves of the gate met with a thunderous clang, they formed one titanic, mailed warrior, whom the goblins called Humongous. His cavernous mouth uttered an unearthly metallic bellow; his eyes glowed. In one hand he wielded an enormous, double-headed ax.

Sarah whimpered. She felt the ground tremble as Humongous, ax raised, detached himself from the doors and stamped toward them. Beside her, she heard Ludo roar, but it was a mere piping sound in comparison to the terrible noise made by this Goliath goblin.

Ambrosius took one look and sensibly bolted. Sir Didymus, dumped on the ground, furiously ordered his steed to return. Ambrosius was having none of it. He lurked behind a buttress.

"Pshaw!" Sir Didymus clicked his fingers in irritation. "Were yon warrior and I to joust with lances, I would make short work of him."

Humongous was not yon now. He had come close enough to aim a massive ax blow at the trio. It missed them, but gashed a great wound in the stone wall. A fountain of sparks spurted from the steel axhead.

The three dodged past Humongous's feet, but he jerked rapidly around and smashed his ax down again with both hands. Screaming, they leaped apart, and the ax hammered the ground between them, burying itself among shattered paving stones. The giant withdrew it effortlessly, and now, crouching, he delivered a scything swing at them. They threw themselves flat, and heard the ax whiz over them with a noise like an ignited rocket.

They saw the ax raised high again, and scuttled for cover to the wall of the courtyard. The descending ax carved a slice off a buttress. Blow followed blow. Each one would have left no more of them than there is of a mosquito squashed on a wall. All that had saved them so far was the inflexible, jerky motion of Humongous's attack, which gave them a split second's forewarning of where the next annihilating crash was aimed. It was only a matter of time before they got it wrong, and Humongous seemed to have all the time he needed, trampling after them around the closed courtyard and evidently not wearied by the atrocious energy of his onslaught.

In a brief moment between one blow and the next, Sir Didymus spotted a movement along the parapet of one wall. "Look!" he panted, and pointed. It was nearly fatal.

"*Watch out!*" Sarah screamed, and the three of them dived simultaneously sideways as the ax whistled and crashed down again, raising a spray of fragmented paving stones.

While Humongous was lining up his next swipe, Sarah saw what the movement on the parapet was. Hoggle was running nimbly along the battlements, toward the arch over the inner gates.

"Hoggle!" Sarah yelled in encouragement, before sprinting between Humongous's feet and out of the way.

It was obscure what assistance Hoggle could bring them, but he was scrambling so urgently up the arch that he clearly had some purpose in mind.

Humongous shifted his feet, like armored tanks, to get in his next blow. In doing so, he positioned himself with his back to the inner gates.

Sarah saw Hoggle, now on top of the arch, crouching, prepared to jump down on the horned helmet of the giant. She covered her face with her hands, terrified, and peeped through her fingers. What hopeless heroism it was in Hoggle, like a fly attacking a locomotive.

With a triumphant shriek, Hoggle landed on Humongous's shoulders.

"Hoggle!" Sarah whispered, as she took off to avoid another thunderous stroke.

Hoggle balanced on one leg, and kicked the giant's helmet. The top half of it flew open, on a hinge. Inside Humongous's head, a tiny goblin in a white lab coat, with eyes staring madly through thick lenses, was feverishly working a bank of levers. Hoggle reached down, grabbed the goblin under the armpits, and hurled him away. He landed haplessly on the flagstones of the courtyard and groped for his smashed spectacles.

Already Hoggle had jumped down inside the giant's head, and was operating the levers there as though he had always been the engineer. Perhaps he did know what he was doing, or perhaps he tugged the levers at random. The result was that Humongous, elbows by his sides and arms raised robotically level, went into a convulsion. His feet did a shuffling sort of dance, his torso swayed from side to side, the ax jerked rapidly up and down, and his neck swiveled faster and faster. Hoggle pulled more levers and then had to make a wild jump for it, as Humongous went careering off blindly, with his ax oscillating and steam spurting from his joints.

Hoggle landed in a heap at Sarah's feet. She helped him up, but had no time to speak to him yet. Humongous was now rampaging around the courtyard like a mad bull, bouncing off the walls. His ax was lashing up and down on a long vertical axis, pulverizing the paving stones when it landed, and crunching into his own back on the reverse stroke.

The giant's random movements eventually brought him back to the inner gates, where he had started. On its next backward swing, the ax penetrated deep into the cleft between two stones in the arch. It stuck there. In consequence, Humongous's next attempt at a mighty downstroke was converted into a terrifying leverage upward of his whole body. He was too heavy for his feet to leave the ground. What might have happened was that the ax could have snapped, or the wall collapsed. What did happen was that Humongous bent at the knees and sagged at the waist, looking like a failed giant hammer-thrower, and little blue sparks shot up and down his armor as his circuits overloaded.

"Are you all right?" Sarah asked Hoggle, bending down to fuss over any bruises he might have.

Hoggle retreated a few paces and stood with his face inclined. "I'm not asking to be forgiven," he said obstinately. "I ain't ashamed of nothin' I did. I don't care what you thinks of me." He was toeing a little stone around with his boot, his eyes fixed on it. "I told you I was a coward. Now you sees I was only tellin' the truth. And I ain't interested in bein' friends…"

"I forgive you, Hoggle," Sarah said, simply.

Hoggle cocked his gnomish head and looked at her from under one bushy eyebrow. "You do?" he asked in a small voice.

Sir Didymus strode across and slapped Hoggle's shoulder. "And I commend thee," he said, with his other hand resting on his staff. "Seldom have I seen such courage. Sir Galahad himself will be impressed when word reaches his ears. We owe to thee our lives. Thou art the fragrant bloom of knightly valor, Sir Hoggle."

"I am?"

Ludo paid his tribute. "Hoggle—Ludo—friends."

"We are?" Hoggle agreed uncertainly.

Sarah had unfastened the string of baubles she had taken from Hoggle in the hedge maze—so long ago, it seemed—and handed them back to him. "Here are your things, Hoggle. And thank you for your help."

Hoggle took the jewels and gazed down at them. Then he looked up with a puckered grin. "Well," he said, and started to stride toward the inner gates, "what are we waiting for?"

Sir Didymus called, "Ambrosius!" His steed poked his nose cautiously around the buttress behind which he had been hiding.

"Ambrosius!" Sir Didymus raised his voice impatiently. Ambrosius did not so much trot as sidle up to his master.

When the knight was mounted up, the party made its way carefully around the massive shape of Humongous. The blue sparks were still fizzing.

Sir Didymus enthusiastically overtook Hoggle and beat upon the inner gates with his staff. Hoggle pushed. Neither of them could get the gates open, but it was an easy job for Ludo. Without Humongous, they were no more than a pair of heavy doors leading to Goblin City.

Jareth was lounging on his throne, propped up on one elbow. Beside him was Toby. Goblins stood around, watching them play together, and wishing that they had Toby to play with. It looked like fun. Jareth would tickle Toby, and whenever he was within range the baby would punch Jareth in the face. The game had been going on for some time.

Jareth chuckled. "Spirited little fellow." In more senses than one, he thought, but why bother to say it when all you've got in the audience are goblins? He nodded. "I think I'll call him Jareth. He's got my eyes."

Toby smacked him in one of them.

"And my disposition," Jareth added.

A goblin came running into the chamber, tripped on a chicken carcass, fell flat on his face, and from there delivered his message. "Your Highness! The girl!"

Jareth glanced up laconically. "What?"

The goblin was picking himself up. "The girl who ate the peach and forgot everything?"

"Yes, yes," Jareth said testily. As though he had had more than one girl on his mind lately. "What of her?"

The goblin's eyes were boggling, and he had one arm flung out behind him, pointing. "She's here."

"Hm?" Jareth stopped tickling Toby and scrutinized the moronic messenger.

"She *here*, your Highness! With the monster, and Sir Didymus, and the gnome who's in your employ."

"Here?"

"They've gotten through the gates."

"*What?*" Jareth barked.

"The girl who ate the peach and—"

"*Yes!*" Jareth's face was working. "She got past Humongous?"

"Yes, your Highness. He's blown his fuses."

"Blown his—where are they?"

"They're on their way to the castle."

Jareth stood up, holding Toby, who wriggled. "Stop her!" the Goblin King commanded. "Call out the guard!"

The goblins milled around the chamber, screeching, "Call out the guard!" at each other.

"Don't mill," Jareth told them. "*Do* something. She must be stopped."

As one goblin, they all dashed for the door.

"Wait!" Jareth shouted. Carrying Toby, he strode over to them and handed the baby to one of them. "Here," he said, "take Jarethkin. She must not get the baby."

The goblin with Toby ran off one way, while the rest rushed off to raise the alarm.

Jareth was left alone. "She must not get the baby," he repeated to himself. "She *must* be stopped."

CHAPTER XVII
SAINTS AND WHISKERS

Goblin City was a shantytown, numbering about ten blocks of ramshackle houses, hiding in each other's shadows, with winding lanes between them. The buildings rose to sharply pointed eaves or conical thatch roofs. The windows penetrating the walls were so higgledy-piggledy that from the outside you might wonder if the houses had floors at all. Most of the buildings were decorated in the Goblin Grotesque style, timber trimmed to a rising point like a waxed mustache, goblinomorphic feet or horns carved into a pediment. The cat-prowled lanes were littered with scraps of food tossed from the windows, and other garbage so rotten that it would be an unsavory task to analyze what it had once been.

The place was huddled in the shadow of the castle, which rose behind it in bonnet-towered and turreted splendor. A wide flight of steps, the main entrance to the castle, faced the inner gates of the courtyard, and must have formed an imposing approach before the shantytown had risen up to interrupt the vista.

Sir Didymus on Ambrosius, Hoggle, Sarah, and Ludo tiptoed

through a marketplace just inside the gates. It was dawn, and the city was apparently fast asleep. Seeing the castle looming up ahead of them, they made their way quietly through the lanes toward it. Here and there they crept past a snoozing goblin, propped against a wall.

Sir Didymus cleared his throat and announced, loudly, "This stealth is alien to my nature."

"Ssshhh!" Sarah told him.

"Quiet, yer windbag!" Hoggle added, in a growl.

"Sorry, fair maid," Sir Didymus apologized, in a voice hardly lowered at all. "I know not the word *fear*."

"I know," Sarah answered, "but *I* do."

"And I does, too," Hoggle added. "Shush!"

Beyond the shantytown, they came into an open square. The steps up to the castle were on the far side. Everything was still eerily quiet. They began to walk softly toward the steps.

Sarah's heart was pounding. "We're going to make it," she whispered.

"Piece of cake," Hoggle told her.

He should have known better. When he had heard her use that phrase, the penalty had been the slashing machine. This time, it was war. A bugle sounded, and from both sides of the square the goblin army suddenly came charging at them, with pounding feet and clanking armor and a weird, ululating war cry. Scores of helmeted heads could be seen scuttling along the lower ramparts of the castle. There was only one thing to do: run for it. And there was only one way to run—back into town.

The armies were issuing from twin corridors, which curved around the sides of the main steps so that their exits faced each other. A platoon of bombardiers trundled a cannon in the vanguard of each army, and as the corridors were on an incline, and the cannons were heavy, and the trundling was enthusiastic, the cannon platoons were going to collide unless they hauled back hard. Which they did. Unavailingly, however, for the press of infantry and cavalry behind them drove them inexorably on. As the four invaders raced for the cover of the town, they heard a stupendous smash, like a thousand empty cans crashing together. They turned around, and watched wave upon wave of the goblin soldiers piling up on top of each other. On the ramparts, an inaudible bugler was red in the face with blowing the charge.

Jareth was standing perpendicular at a window of the castle, watching the action. He winced, almost imperceptibly.

Hoggle led Sarah, Ludo, and the mounted Sir Didymus in a sprint along the mazy lanes of the town. Goblin heads popped out of windows above them to watch. Sir Didymus was protesting, "We must stand and fight them face to face. It is the only honorable…"

Hoggle suddenly stopped, his arms spread wide in warning. The rest halted behind him. At the far end of the street, a detachment of goblins appeared facing them, spiky with spears.

"Uh-oh," Sarah muttered. "This could be it."

"Fear not, sweet damsel," Sir Didymus told her. "These puny goblins are no match for Sir Didymus." He raised his staff, and was about to charge the army singlehanded when Ambrosius wheeled around and bolted again. This time, his rider managed to stay in the saddle and, after touring the streets, brought Ambrosius back to where they had started.

Sarah called urgently from a doorway. "In here!"

She had found a deserted house in which to make a stand. It was built like a tower.

Reluctantly, Sir Didymus dismounted and led Ambrosius inside. Sarah slid the bolt. She was grinning with excitement. However extreme the peril they were in, nothing would ever be as daunting as the old junk woman. "You hold the doorway," she told Sir Didymus. "Hoggle and I will guard that window. And you, Ludo—up on the roof."

Ludo nodded obediently. "Ludo—up." He climbed the winding rungs of the stairs.

"Look out!" Sarah cried suddenly. On the wall of the room, she had seen goblin shadows, snouted and horned, cast through the window by the rising sun. Sir Didymus at once took up his on-guard position beside the door. Sarah and Hoggle stood by a dresser full of china.

Sarah called up the staircase. "Ludo, are you ready?"

"Ludo—ready."

A goblin smashed the window with his pike, and stuck his head inside to see who was in there. Sarah, standing to one side of the window, brought a dinner plate down upon his head. He collapsed onto the windowsill and rolled outside.

Another took his place. Another plate served the same purpose.

At once, a third head was poked in. This one had time to peer at the defenders. "Hoggle!" the goblin exclaimed. "You used to be with us."

"Yes," Hoggle agreed, and broke a teapot on the goblin's helmeted head.

Another ugly head took its turn at the window, and another, and as fast as their pointed ears and jagged teeth appeared they were stunned by Sarah or Hoggle.

Sir Didymus was watching with mixed feelings. He had to hand it to the girl, she was doughty, and she might make a decent commander of horse one day. On the other hand, she had posted her most valorous knight inside a bolted wooden door, where nothing at all was going to happen. Inexperience, that was all it was. He was wondering whether to disobey orders and join them at the window when an axhead shaped like a trefoil splintered the door. Through the crack it had made, he saw mad red eyes watching him and heard voices talking rapidly.

This was more like it. He squared up. Then, through the crack, he saw half a dozen goblins charging with a battering ram. In a trice, he slid the bolt back and opened the door. As the ram went past him at full tilt he dealt with each of its bearers adroitly with a thrust of his trusty staff. "Have at thee!" he hollered excitedly. "En garde, sirrah!"

He slammed the door shut and bolted it again, and was trying to use the battering ram to shore up the splintered door when it was burst open by a fresh squad of goblins. He had no time to grab his staff. They leaped upon him, pinioned him face down to the ground, and, holding his hair, began to bash his nose on the floor. After a while, they paused to examine their work.

"Ha!" Sir Didymus shouted tauntingly. "Had enough, have ye? Craven curs, how little it takes to subdue varlets such as ye are!"

They started to give him another bashing for that, but Sarah had seen what was going on. A well-aimed chamber pot sent the goblins flying, and in a moment Sir Didymus was standing over them. "Saints and whiskers!" he exclaimed. "Is it worth splintering my staff to dispatch the likes of ye?"

Sarah and Hoggle were still holding the window, but their reserve of crockery was running low, and the horde of goblins was not abating. When there were no more dinner plates, jugs, or soup bowls, they had to use teacups and saucers, but sometimes it took two of those to deal with each goblin.

Another one of them had time to recognize Hoggle. "What have we done to *you?*" the goblin asked.

"Not me," Hoggle replied. "Her—you stole her baby brother."

"So we stole a baby! That's what goblins *do.* You know that, Hog—"

His sentence was ended by a soup tureen that Hoggle had been saving for a special occasion.

On the roof of the tower, Ludo was showered with spears. He simply ducked below the parapet. Then a detachment of commando goblins stormed the outside walls of the tower, clambering up ladders with the idea of overwhelming Ludo. He was not readily overwhelmable, kicking them down to the ground one by one as they reached the top of the ladders and peered over the parapet. The artillery was called up. From a cannon, a goblin with a spiked helmet was fired at Ludo. The outcome was that the goblin's helmet was impaled in the mud wall of a nearby house, leaving him stuck out behind it, flapping his limbs.

Sir Didymus was listening keenly. Outside the door, he could hear two goblins conversing. "She's got brains," one said.

"Yes," the other replied. "I could do with brains like hers."

"So could I," the first said. "To eat!"

Sir Didymus was incensed. To hear them impugning so beautiful a damsel without mercy was more than his knightly honor could tolerate. Throwing open the door and leaping on Ambrosius's back, he cried, "Ye Goths and Vandals! Have at ye, then, for the foul blasphemers that ye are of a maiden's virtue."

Sarah looked across and saw Sir Didymus level his staff and charge out. "No!" she cried. It was too late.

Sir Didymus came back a moment later, on his back, head first. Ambrosius followed at a gallop.

The peerless knight-at-arms was up and at them in an instant. This time, Ambrosius bolted with him all around the town again, until they came face to face with a bristling line of spears. More spears appeared behind them in the narrow lane.

"Don't worry, Ambrosius," Sir Didymus told him. "I think we've got them surrounded."

With a dazzlingly rapid series of thrusts, parries, and flicks, he disarmed all the adversaries in front of him, and charged triumphantly forward into a low porch beam, which unseated him from the saddle. By the time he was on his feet, he was hemmed in by spear points.

"Ha!" he snarled. "Can't take any more, eh? Very well. Throw down your weapons, and I'll see to it that you're well treated."

As the spears came down at him, he ran up one of them and vaulted back into the saddle, which unfortunately was no longer there, Ambrosius having once again taken the sensible course of action.

Meanwhile, Sarah had had an idea. "Ludo," she shouted, "call the rocks!"

The noise of the battle was too loud for Ludo, at the top of the house, to hear her. She would have to go up to him. "Hoggle, retreat!" she called. "Up the stairs."

"You first," he called back.

She did as he said. Hoggle followed her.

Sir Didymus, hard pressed, ran into the house just in time to cover their retreat. He came up the stairs backward, ceding one step at a time, fending off his attackers with cut and passado.

Sarah raced up to the top of the tower. "Ludo," she panted. "Call the rocks. Call the rocks, Ludo."

Ludo did not need the second bidding. He threw his great head back, closed his eyes, and bellowed longer and louder than an alpine horn.

The tower quivered and the earth shuddered. A distant rumbling was heard. Bits fell off the castle walls.

While they were waiting for the rocks to arrive, their immediate position was perilous. Sir Didymus could not hold back the invaders for much longer. Ludo had kicked away the scaling ladders, and so they were going to be trapped at the top of the tower unless there was some way down the outside. Not even Ludo's friends the rocks could help them up there.

Sarah looked over the parapet. All the goblins were congregated at the front of the house, struggling to get in after those who were forcing Sir Didymus back. The lane behind the house was empty, which gave Sarah an idea.

Just below the tower roof she had passed a room with two beds in it. The goblins had not yet advanced that far. She ran down. "Hold them back for as long as you can, Sir Didymus," she called.

" 'Twill be the greatest pleasure of my life, fair maid," he called back up to her.

Swiftly, Sarah knotted sheets and blankets together in a rope. Then she ran back up to the tower roof, tied one end of the rope to a column of the parapet and threw the rest over the side. She looked down and was relieved to see it reached nearly to the ground. "You first, Hoggle," she said.

He hesitated. "I'm a coward."

"No, you're not."

He paused, almost smiling. "You're right. I'm not. Funny, I always thought I was." He grasped the rope, stood on the parapet, and shinned down to the ground. Then he held the rope to anchor it for Sarah. She followed him down.

"Ludo!" she called. "You next! Tell Sir Didymus to come after you."

Seeing the bulk of Ludo loom above the parapet, she crossed her fingers and prayed that the rope would bear his weight. She could barely watch.

It was all right. Ludo came down, a little too fast, scorching his paws, but he landed safely on the ground.

Now it was time for Sir Didymus to make good his escape. The three of them, their heads craned back, saw the tiny puissant chevalier come onto the parapet with his back turned and his staff arm working hard. With his free hand he took hold of the rope and let himself a few inches down the outside of the tower. Then they saw him raise his staff and unhitch the rope from the parapet. He plummeted.

Sarah pressed her hands to her cheeks. Her mouth opened in horror.

But the resourceful knight knew what he was doing. With his staff hand he grabbed the other side of the sheet, and spread his arms wide. The air filled the sheet, and he parachuted gently down beside his friends.

Sarah used the breath she had been holding to gasp, "Sir Didymus! What did you do that for?"

"Prithee, sweet damsel," Sir Didymus answered, "wilt thou raise thy lovely eyes aloft?"

Sarah looked up, and saw a ring of baffled goblin faces staring angrily down from the top of the tower.

"Thou wouldst not have wished them to join our company, wouldst thou?" Sir Didymus asked, his eyes twinkling.

During their escape, the rumbling of the rocks had grown into an oceanic roar. They came rolling across the plain by the hundreds, answering Ludo's call, and when they hit the outer walls of the city they built themselves up until the next to arrive could just roll up the slope and vault inside. Soon they filled the streets, knocking goblins down like tenpins and ruthlessly pursuing those who fled. There was no hiding place. The boulders crashed through the doors of houses where the army had taken cover, and when the goblins jumped spread-eagled out of windows, the rocks were close behind them. Whole platoons of goblins were walled up by rocks stacked against doors.

The artillery commander, knowing no other way to fight, ordered the cannon to be loaded and discharged at the invaders. Just as the fuse was ignited, a rock stuffed itself into the mouth of the cannon, which exploded, leaving the commander a blackened, ragged scarecrow.

Sarah led her friends back through the chaotic town to the square in front of the castle. A couple of stray halberdiers boldly confronted them before the steps. From behind them, Sarah heard a loud rumbling. She whipped around and screamed. A boulder was rolling at them. It leapfrogged them and dropped *splat* on the halberdiers.

"Rocks—friends," Ludo remarked, with a touch of pride.

At the top of the steps was a tall, narrow, grotesquely carved door, the ceremonial entrance. Sarah pushed at it. It was locked and solid.

Ludo walked past her and broke the door down as though it were matchwood.

Inside the castle, a grand corridor ran ahead of them, and at the far end of it, through an open door, they could see the throne, with the vulture squatting above it.

"Toby," Sarah whispered, and ran to fetch him. If Jareth were there, he could not stop her now. Nothing could.

The chamber was deserted. In the middle of it was a cradle, empty. The clock showed three minutes to thirteen. On his perch, the vulture shifted from foot to foot. He opened his beak and made a noise like ghastly laughter.

CHAPTER XVIII
SEEMING

"Toby," Sarah whispered again, gazing down at the empty cradle.

Sir Didymus was looking from her face to the cradle. He lifted the blanket and the pillow, searching beneath them, and shook his head. "An exceptionally small knight is Sir Tobias. I cannot even see him."

"He's gone," Sarah said. "Jareth has taken him."

The vulture made a dry cackling noise.

Sarah knew that Jareth would not have abandoned the castle. He had to be here somewhere, and so had Toby. The sole exit from the chamber, apart from the way they had come, was a flight of stairs to one side of the throne. She could not see where it led because the passage turned a corner, but a lovely glowing light was emanating from it. "That's the only way he could have gone," Sarah said.

She ran toward it, taking care to avoid stepping on the half-gnawed chicken bones, rotting tomatoes, squashed pears, and other garbage that littered the floor. Sir Didymus, Hoggle, and Ludo ran after her.

"No," she said, when she reached the first stair. She turned around and told her friends, "I... I have to face him alone."

Sir Didymus, already rehearsing his lunge and parry as he ran, was disconcerted. "Why?" he asked.

"Because…" It was a good question. "Because that's the way it's done," Sarah replied.

"Who says?" Hoggle asked.

"They all do," Sarah told him. "The stories, all of them."

The three of them regarded her for some time. Seeing the disappointment on their faces, Sarah felt wretched. But she knew that she was right.

At length, Sir Didymus said, slowly, "Well, if that is the way 'tis done, then, that is how thou must needs do it." He raised his staff and squinted along it. "But shouldst thou have need of us…"

"Yes," Hoggle added, "if you need us…"

"I'll call," Sarah promised. "Thank you. All of you." She smiled, feeling awkward with gratitude.

Then she turned and ran up the stairs, toward the glowing light.

It was a long staircase and turned through several angles. She was puffing by the time she reached the top and emerged onto a stone platform. What she saw took all her breath away.

Above, below, or around her—which, she could not tell—was a vast stone hall, with so many staircases, balconies, windows, and doorways at different heights and odd angles to each other that she had no idea what was up or down, near or far, inside or out, backward or forward. Planes reversed themselves as you watched them, receding corners suddenly jutted out, rising steps inverted themselves, floors became ceilings, and walls turned into precipices. In this room, it seemed that the law of gravity had been repealed, and perspective had seven dimensions. If there had been water, if would have seemed to flow uphill. She felt sick and giddy, and had to cling to a pillar to remain upright. "It's impossible," she whispered to herself. As long as she went on looking at the hall, it went on altering. Does it still go on altering, she wondered dizzily, when no one is looking at it?

With her back to the wall, she edged along the platform. If I take it step by step, she was thinking, I will get there. If there *is* a there. She edged along, hoping that it *was* along and not up or past or through, until she came to a point that she was quite certain was where she had started. Yes, there was the top of the staircase behind her. She began to edge the other way, until she heard a voice from somewhere below. She knew whose voice it was.

"I've been expecting you," it said.

With a deep breath, she inched to the edge of the platform. Beyond her, apparently sitting on a vertical wall, was Jareth.

"Where's Toby?" Sarah asked.

"He's safe. In my keeping."

"You're not keeping him."

"Oh. And why not?"

"I have come this far. I am here."

Jareth chuckled. "Sheer luck."

"I am here. Give me Toby back."

"You have understood nothing," Jareth told her. "You have answered none of the Labyrinth's riddles. You don't even know what the questions were."

"That wasn't our bargain."

Jareth threw back his head and laughed. "There, just as I told you. You have understood nothing."

"You are wrong. I have come to understand one thing very well. You are just putting on a show of confidence. It doesn't take me in anymore. You are frightened, Jareth."

"So are you."

"Yes."

For a few seconds, they were watching each other's eyes.

Then Jareth began to move, all over the seven perspectives, and Sarah watched him as he moved. He seemed to walk along ceilings and climb descending stairs. He danced on high walls. And as he moved he called to her. "You are cruel, Sarah. We are well matched, you and I. I need your cruelty, just as you need mine."

Watching him, Sarah felt her knees start to wobble. She had fallen for his trick. She had no idea now whether she was looking up or down, whether the platform where she stood was solid or void. Everything switched continually, like a photographic negative at an angle to the light. She held her arms out for balance, but it was no good. She stumbled, her head spinning, and felt herself topple. She landed on a ceiling, and tried to adjust her senses. Shakily, she stood up.

Then she saw Toby. He was crawling up a flight of stairs, still in his striped pajamas.

"Toby!" she called.

The baby did not respond.

"Toby!" she shouted.

The only answer she got was Jareth's laughter.

Somehow, she had to reach Toby. She began to work her way down a flight of stairs. A movement below her caught her attention. She peered beneath the stairs and saw Jareth walking parallel to her, apparently upside down, like a reflection in ice. Or maybe she was upside down. She ran to get away from him, to get to Toby. Jareth mirrored her wherever she went. She ran along a balcony, and suddenly he appeared at the far end of it, upright. She turned, ran back, and fell. She landed with a bruising thud. Jareth was watching her, laughing.

"I will reach him," Sarah said to Jareth.

Instead of answering, Jareth produced a crystal ball and tossed it up a flight of stairs. Sarah's eyes followed it, and she saw it land near Toby, who was happily climbing on hands and knees up another staircase.

"Toby!" she cried in alarm.

The baby was fascinated by the bouncing ball. He reached for it, and when it passed him he scuttled after it. Sarah saw him approaching the edge of a precipitous fall.

"No!" she called out. "*Oh, no!* Toby!"

Toby went over the edge and crawled down the vertical wall, still chasing the ball, which was bouncing around crazily in defiance of all laws of motion.

Sarah blinked. It was impossible. Jareth laughed.

She started to follow a line of stairs that went in the direction of Toby. As she drew near him, the baby crawled after the ball in another plane, leaving her stranded. She followed him again, and the same thing happened, and again. He was moving on an axis with which she could not intersect. And everywhere he crawled, he seemed to be at risk of falling from a balcony, or tumbling all the way down a flight of stone stairs.

Suddenly, Jareth appeared behind her. He laid his hands on her shoulders and spun her around. She was too weak to resist him. His face, as he looked into hers, was amused. It said: It's been a fine game, Sarah, and now it's time to finish playing, because you cannot ever win.

In the corner of her eye, she saw a small movement. Toby was crawling toward a window ledge. She shrugged Jareth's hands from her shoulders and stared at her brother. There could be no optical doubt about it this time. Outside the window, birds were flying in the sunlight, and Toby was clambering up onto the ledge. Between her and the baby was a vast space of the hall. He was teetering on the ledge now, trying to stand up. She could not run to him, even supposing she were able to find a path to him through the deceiving planes. It was possible, she could not be sure, that he was below her, and that she could reach him with a jump: a jump so deep that she would crack every bone in her body.

Jareth was smiling triumphantly at her. This was how her quest ended. If he could not keep the baby, nor would she. She watched Toby totter on his precarious perch, and a small cry came from her lips.

She closed her eyes and jumped.

When she opened her eyes, she was not sure where she was. It could have been another part of the hall. She thought she recognized it, but could not place it.

Yet something had changed. Near her was an ogee window, without glass, and through it she could see the upper half of one wing of the castle. It was in ruins, the cladding stones mostly gone, grass growing in the gaps they'd left. The turret roofs had collapsed, and brambles were reaching for the throat of the tower. Within the castle, where she was, she heard in the air the humming that she had come to associate with Jareth, but it had a hollow ring to it, something forlorn, like music in an abandoned house. In the crack between two flagstones where she lay she saw that weeds had started to push their way through. She stood up and looked around. There was no sign of Toby.

Jareth stepped out from a shadowy archway, wearing a faded, threadbare cloak. His face looked older, drawn. In his blond mane was a trace of gray.

How long had she been here? She detected no change in herself.

Jareth was waiting for her with his arms folded. She advanced upon him. "Give me the child," she said.

He paused before answering. "Sarah—beware. I have been generous until now, but I can be cruel."

"Generous!" She advanced another step. "What have you done that was generous?"

"Everything. I have done everything you wanted." He took a pace back, into the shadow of the archway. "You asked that the child be taken. I took him. You cowered before me. I was frightening."

Taking another step away from her, he gestured in the air. "I have reordered time," he told her. The thirteen-hour clock had appeared, floating above his head. Its hands were whirling around. "I have turned the world upside down."

Sarah continued to advance upon him, her arms outstretched. He retreated deeper into the shadows.

"And I have done it all for *you*," he said with a shake of his head. "I am exhausted from living up to your expectations. Isn't that generous? Stay back!" He raised his hands as though to fend her off and took another pace away from her. In a louder voice, he repeated, "Stay back!"

Sarah's lips were parted. "Through dangers untold and hardships unnumbered, I have fought my way here to the castle beyond the Goblin City—"

"Listen!" said a goblin, one of a nest in a dark corner of the castle.

Jareth was retreating step by step up a staircase behind the archway.

Sarah continued to advance, into the archway.

"—to take back the child you have stolen," she recited. "For my will is as strong as yours—"

"Stop!" Jareth raised the palm of his hand to her. "Wait! Sarah, look—look what I can offer you." He raised his left arm and made a large gesture with his hand. A glowing crystal ball appeared in it. He spun it around in his fingers, smiled wanly, and said, "It will show you your dreams. You remember."

Sarah took another step.

"—and my kingdom as great—"

"She's going to say it," a goblin hissed.

"She's going to say the words," gabbled another, agitatedly.

The stairs behind Jareth were descending now, and he backed slowly down them as Sarah stood above him. "I ask so little," he said, spinning the crystal. "Just believe in me, and you can have everything you want... everything you have ever dreamed of... your dreams, Sarah..."

She was frowning, and had halted her advance. "...and my kingdom as great...," she said. "Damn!"

A goblin shook his head decisively. "That's not it. Never."

"Sshh!" said another.

Sarah's fists were clenched white. She was thinking frantically. What were her right words?

Jareth took a step toward her. He needed her belief in him. "Just fear me and love me," he told her in a gentle voice, "and do as I say, and I... I will be your slave." He stretched his hand out toward her, and took another step back up the stairs.

"Nah." A goblin shook his hideous head. "Doesn't look like it now, does it?"

Jareth's fingers were close to Sarah's face.

She stood where she was, and swallowed. "Kingdom as great...," she muttered, "...kingdom as great..." She saw the crystal spinning in his fingers, and felt on her lips the warmth of his outstretched hand. She gasped, and, from some inspired recess of her mind, the words came, blurted out.

"You have no power over me."

"*No!*" Jareth screamed.

"No!" the goblins exclaimed, astounded.

A clock began to strike.

Jareth tossed the crystal ball up into the air, where it hovered, a bubble. Sarah looked at it, and saw Jareth's face, distorted, on the shifting, iridescent surface. Gently, it drifted down toward her. She reached out fascinated fingers for it and, as she touched the bubble with her fingertips, it burst. A mist of water atoms floated down the air toward Jareth.

But she saw Jareth had disappeared. She heard his voice, for a last time, moaning, "Sarah… Sarah…" His empty cloak was settling onto the ground. A beam of light picked out a little cloud of dust motes rising from it.

The clock continued to strike.

With a last, slow flutter, the cloak lay still. From beneath it, as the clock struck for the twelfth time, a white owl flew out and circled over Sarah.

Tears were trickling down her cheeks.

CHAPTER XIX
GOOD NIGHT

Sarah closed her eyes to stem the tears and brushed her cheeks with the palms of her hands. "I must stop this habit of crying," she said aloud, as a distraction from her sadness. "I must also stop gasping, gulping, trembling, shouting, and generally going over the top when…" Then she remembered that she had not found Toby again, and she opened her eyes in alarm.

The white owl was still flapping above her, but in other respects the scene had changed. She was standing on the staircase of her home, and it was dark outside.

She raised her eyes to look at the owl. It circled her for a last time, found an open window and flew out into the night. Then she was running up the stairs two at a time, shouting, "Toby! Toby!"

He was in his crib, fast asleep. She could not help but pick him up and cuddle him. He opened his eyes dozily, thought about crying, but decided that he was in good enough shape without it, so he smiled instead. Sarah picked up Launcelot from the floor and put the teddy bear in his arms, saying, "Here you are, Toby. He's yours." Then she tucked him into his crib again. He went straight to sleep.

She stayed there with him for a long time, watching him breathe peacefully, with Launcelot in his arms.

Back in her own room, the full moon was shining outside the window. She left the curtains open, to see it. If she went to bed quickly, it would still be shining in when she turned the light out. The alarm clock by her bed showed that the time was after midnight. Her parents would be back from the show any minute now.

She sat at her dressing table and picked up a hairbrush, but her attention wandered to the photographs she had around the mirror, her mother and Jeremy, smiling at each other like young lovers, the signed posters, the gossip stories about a romantic attachment. Deliberately, she began to remove one picture after another from the mirror. She glanced at each before putting it away in a drawer.

On the dressing table one picture remained, of her father and mother and herself, aged ten. Sarah straightened the picture. Then she went to get the music box and put it in the drawer along with the pictures and clippings, shoved far back.

Downstairs, she heard the front door open and close. Her stepmother called, "Sarah?"

She didn't answer at once. She was holding her copy of *The Labyrinth*. "Sarah?"

"Wait," Sarah whispered. "I am closing a chapter of my life. Just wait." She paused, and added, still in a whisper, "Please." She put the book in the drawer with all the rest, and stood with her hand on it there.

"Sarah!"

Sarah left it a moment, then called back, "Yes. Yes, I'm here." She looked at the drawer, and sighed. "Welcome back," she called.

"*What?*" Her stepmother, taking her coat off downstairs, paused, puzzled. "What did you say?" she called up.

Sarah opened her mouth, and closed it again. Once was enough, she thought. Once was all right. Any more would be overweening. I nearly overwent there, she smiled to herself, and pushed the drawer shut.

She straightened up, and on the dark window saw her reflection against the moonlight. Behind her reflection was Ludo.

"Ludo—good-bye—Sarah," he said.

She spun around with a cry of joy. The room was empty.

She checked the window again. Sir Didymus was there.

"And remember, sweetest damsel, shouldst thou ever have need..."

"I'll call," she told him. She glanced around at the room again. Empty, of course.

Sir Didymus was hurrying back into the windowpane. "I forgot to say, also, that if ever thou shouldst think on marriage..."

"I understand," Sarah told him. "Good-bye, brave Sir Didymus."

He faded. Sarah kept her eyes on the window. She did not have long to wait. Hoggle popped up from behind the bed. "Yes, if you ever need us... for any reason *at all*..." He stared at her from under his bushy eyebrows, and started to fade.

"Hoggle," Sarah said, "I need you. I need you all."

"Sometimes," the Wise Man observed, "to need is... to let go."

"Oh, *wow!*" said his hat. "And that's just for starters."

Outside the dark window, the white owl had been perched with his claws hooked on a branch, an effigy of watching and waiting. Now he swooped away over the park, on silent velvet wings, up toward the full moon. Nobody saw him, white in the moonlight, black against the stars.

THE END

BRIAN FROUD
ILLUSTRATION GALLERY

On the following pages are never-before-seen conceptual designs for the goblins and creatures of *Labyrinth*, created by Jim Henson's longtime collaborator and world-renowned fantasy illustrator Brian Froud between 1984 and 1985. Froud was integral to the conceptualization of *Labyrinth*—and a number of his designs were eventually collected into *The Goblins of Labyrinth*, a gorgeous art book that took readers deeper into Brian's creative process on the film.

The drawings collected here come from the conceptual stage of the film, when Brian and Jim were working with Jim Henson's Creature Shop to build the world of *Labyrinth* and to translate Brian's drawings from the page to fully-operational puppets. These conceptual designs have never been seen publicly, and have remained in The Jim Henson Company Archives since Froud created them. As part of Archaia's ongoing effort to document the legacy of Jim Henson, we're proud to present a deeper look at the genius of Brian Froud, and to honor his collaboration with Jim on one of the best-loved fantasy films of all time.

Stephen Christy
Los Angeles, California

pegs

TWISTS AND TURNS
JIM HENSON'S CONCEPTS FOR LABYRINTH, 1983

In the week before the December 17, 1982 release of Jim Henson's first fantasy film, *The Dark Crystal*, select audiences were treated to exclusive premiere screenings in New York, Los Angeles, and San Francisco. After the third screening, Jim, his conceptual designer Brian Froud, and Froud's wife and puppet builder Wendy rode away in a limousine from the Institute of Fine Arts where the film had been shown and reflected on their shared accomplishment. As Froud remembered almost a quarter-century later, Jim was already proposing that they start discussions about a second film together. Froud was enthusiastic and suggested a story with goblins, perhaps involving a passage through a labyrinth. The idea appealed to Jim; it tapped into his interest in mythology and folklore (inspired by his daughter Lisa's studies at Harvard University) and his affection for enchanted journeys like those in his literary favorites, *Alice's Adventures in Wonderland* and *The Wizard of Oz*.

The Frouds returned to their home in England, and Brian began a series of watercolors depicting his visual concepts, starting with a baby amidst a group of goblins. Jim took a much needed vacation, spending two weeks in Aspen, Colorado with his family, and then began a two and a half month tour promoting the international release of *The Dark Crystal*. There was added excitement surrounding the premiere of the first season of *Fraggle Rock* on HBO and the CBC, and, along with promotional appearances, Jim spent a few days "fraggling" (as noted in his journal) in the studio in Toronto. Given his restless imagination, there was no doubt that Jim, despite everything else, was also tapping some of his creative energy to think about his conversation with Froud. Meetings in London in late January followed, and Brian and Wendy Froud, Jim and writer Dennis Lee began formulating their fantasy. At the beginning of March, Jim carved out some time to set down his first concepts on paper.

Flying from Japan to Australia, Jim opened a cloth-bound blank book and inscribed his name and contact information. He dated the first page, noting that he was in Tokyo, and on the facing page drew a dragon-like creature whose scales resembled a maze. He tried out a few titles: *The Labyrinth. The Maze. The Labyrinth Twist. The Tale of the Labyrinth.* Jim knew that beyond inventive settings and characters, a compelling story should be the principal concern as he developed his next film. But instead of starting with a storyline, Jim couldn't resist beginning his exploration with descriptions of specific personalities, locations, and especially "episodes" – moments in the story when the main character, called Taya at the beginning and eventually dubbed Sarah, would be challenged with a riddle or needed to escape a dangerous and strange situation in order to advance in the labyrinth.

Jim immediately thought of an interaction between a King, his jester and a giant Buddha. Coming to the project as both director and performer, he was already envisioning the camera angles and how specific mechanisms could give his characters realistic motion. He described a room full of snakes and suggested a way to have them slither along using a system of interior ropes pulled in opposite directions. One idea seemed to fulfill a puppeteer's fantasy: "something with six fingers," he wrote. How useful that would be for someone in Jim's line of work! He wanted his players to encounter surreal situations, with reverse perspectives and optical illusions. With one word, "Escher," he laid out an idea for what would turn out to be one of the most visually compelling sequences of the film: Jareth singing "Within You" in the staircase-filled room inspired by the drawings of Dutch artist M.C. Escher. Jim reminded himself that there were unlimited ways to create surprising visuals and noted, "Find chemist" to explore the properties of smoke, and asked himself how dangerous it would be to exploit the intriguing qualities of a puddle of mercury.

While Jim instinctively imagined the creature-driven incidents and effects first, he did not neglect the importance of story development and began making notes to that end. Going back to his existential experimental works from the 1960s like *Time Piece*, *The Cube* and *Tale of Sand*, Jim grappled with issues of illusion versus reality and how a person reacts when confronted with perplexing situations. He noted a need to research the historical meaning behind a labyrinth, and eventually expanded his study, having colleagues pull material on visual humor, puzzles, magic, screen icons, and archetypes of classic fairy tales. Perhaps informed by his work on *Fraggle Rock*, Jim began to formulate a philosophy for the film that focused on forgiveness and understanding, emphasizing the ways we learn to understand other people's points of view.

Jim continued to add to his notebook during the spring and summer of 1983. He had recruited Toronto Poet Laureate (and *Fraggle Rock* lyricist) Dennis Lee to help develop a narrative. After several meetings, much correspondence, and with inspiration from Brian Froud's artwork, Lee produced a "poetic novella" outlining a coming-of-age story set in a world of goblins, hairy beasts and animated masonry. Jim consulted with numerous people about the story, ranging from his in-house creative team and the Fraggle producer Larry Mirkin to a Vanity Fair editor and the film's executive producer George Lucas. Lee's novella became the basis for the screenplay written by Terry Jones and Laura Phillips which, in turn, became the basis for A.C.H. Smith's novelization.

With his small notebook, Jim had started on a path, uncertain where it would lead in terms of filmmaking. "After all," Jim said in the film's production notes, "life is a kind of Labyrinth, with all its twists and turns, its straight paths and its occasional dead ends." Lucky for us, Jim's handwritten wanderings led to laughter, imaginative thinking, and to that magic time between sleeping and dreaming when anything is possible.

Karen Falk
Archives Director, The Jim Henson Company
Long Island City, New York

— Jim HENSON —

NEW YORK CITY
212-794-2400
LONDON
431-1885
431-

March 1983

the Labyrinth

the Maze

the Labyrinth Twist

The Tale of the Labyrinth

Random
incidents in
the LABYRINTH

King + Jester get
themselves locked in cage —

large hand grasps top of
cage — cut to wide shot

also able
to hold in the
hand

· large Buddha type figure
lifts cage — use 6" figures of
K + Jester — make radio controlled
 miniatures

 large figure sits squeezed into
space + no words — very deep
synthesized voice

use arms inside foam arms

pair of ropes
inside solid tube
of foam - covered with
cast scales - able to pull
the ropes against each other
for internal coily movement
also have wires to attach to
rope to anchor to foam

Snake – serpent chamber

an area filled with serpents –
generally very large –
  operated from behind –
latex skin over ropes

Surrealism

encounter statues of themselves?

symbolism — keys / clues —
word keys?

Things which mean something
keep turning up

reverse perspective? Escher

play with sizes — small and
very dangerous?

— humor — sometimes strange

places to change

— start out as one thing — shift
into something else —

open space — desert — becomes
closed in — claustrophobic

— use some natural locations
take with us doorways —
architectural details — carved pieces

huge face appears in the
landscape — as part of mountain

Oxford Scientific

insects – aerial image

pinhole camera

flying ray-type fish

RESOURCE → RESEARCH

What is the meaning of a labyrin

what kinds of puzzles are possible

What can we learn about ancient labyrinths?

Games – a la tic tac toe – don't need explanation

Riddles

THINGS to Remember —

puddles of mercury
   can travel around — also
   waterfall or trickle of
   mercury? how dangerous?

Disney Epcot spurt fountains —
short jets

find chemist — what can he
discover for us — smoke —

walking tree — other things with
multiple people inside

King + Jester to be real
with masks — develop
unique walk — movement
not natural

larger version of Jester could
enable us to put an acrobat in
the figure — possibly a child — only
go up 50% or so

King ~~Jester~~ could carry staff —
capable of some magic —
+ changes to award?

Jester carries stick with head
on it — makes comments —
or wa wa — woo woo
at inappropriate moments

as our guys touch space - hole
slides out / - other player moves by
rock sliding towards us.

perhaps Jester plays - wins - door
opens - / along line of win ?
he goes aha + goes thru.
     King steps forward but
door slams in his face - he
plays + loses

Play Game

piecer
in
store →

Carvings that move —

door

face

Elaborately carved Gallery
of faces —

faces to be manipulated from
behind — could act as a chorus
possibly ask a riddle — needs
to be solved —

the door could be carved

an area filled with jewels —
pluck one + a drop of blood
appears —

area of dry ice smoke —

King walks ~~here~~ ~~to~~ waist deep
Jester's head pops up from time
to time — play for humor —

sound of splash — he yells for help —
King pokes with his staff to find him

fog could blow away & we're
in a completely different
environment

this would mean we stay
with this scene - then go
into the maze with King &
Jester after the court
realizes & kidnapping scene, etc.

—AS THEY GO INTO
LABYRINTH—

we see a faint transparent
image of themselves shrink down
to an inch tall or so - King & Jester
talk - "what is happening?"

the background people -
shot from floor level thru
diffussion - are all in slow motion
wild jubilation-type things going
on - the Queen dancing - the baby
throwing food etc -

then transparent version of
black King/weird person comes out
of his body & speaks to them -
(he stays large) The game is
now real - picks them up -
(huge hand) and drops them into
the game - perhaps in the slo-
mo background we see the queen
notice the King - do a take then
cut to real time - >

invisible or
nearly invisible

MUSIC

have Trevor work with
Medieval instruments + synthesizer

totally different sound - back to the
ideas that we were working with before

What is philosophy of film
what are we trying to say
attitude toward | God
| Religion
| Woman

forgiveness — understanding —
acceptance of other POV

King ⟵⟶ Jester

Spirit   Matter

opposites

Shape-changer being all the foes

creature made of
flames

---

multi creatures — in
some narrow claustrophobic
area — like rats or rodents
or maybe some area populated
by _lots_ of creatures

Front projection — see edge —
another image on back
— then 3-D creature charges

age — 35 years later
illusion

conversations with Death / Wisdom

SHOP

Mike McCormick — Linda
Tad
Rollie — Art? — Jane G
Sherry
Wendy
David B
Lyle — Aug.
              Connie.

Amy
Bob P.

Elliot Scott — designer

CAST

Simon McCorkendale
Michael Gothard (Jaws 3-D)
Kevin Klein

Girl in El Nido — w/ small man

Names

Hoggle   Wirt

Shape Shifter — Shape Changer
(King of Goblins)

Baby

Ludo
Didymus

Jareth — King of Goblins
  becomes Torquil

Sleeping environment

faces in rocks — trees — evil
place woos her to sleep —
treacherous

Ragged Band

Great Beast STRONG

small + feisty

humorous conjurer — King of Goblins

crowds of people in FIRST
world — [j]ammed in narrow
streets — all masked?

Labyrinth represents all pitfalls
of the world above

cycle of King above reborn in babe

Cinderella type – others better qualified

encounter other people who ~ other versions of herself?
didn't make it through the Lab.

Time Clock w/ Goblin King +
baby — to Death?

set up situations — make mistakes

something terrible happens to her —
warts on face?

she has illusions
that get destroyed

Saying no sends her through —
yes would have meant she was the
wrong one.

Someone gives her a stick/staff

May 9
meeting

animals — unique strange
cuddly—kitten — other animal to do
Moorish castles? this

Zoo person consultant

dance —

get piper from Dark Crystal
to see what he could play

Music

Song by Torquil — w/ pan pipes

dance of death

lullaby for baby

July 25, (83)

the central castle should be taller
so as to be seen from different
places en route — could look
quite close at the beginning

WORLDS

Scrambled Senses
First World - pick up somebody?
Medieval Town   Island
                      Didymus - belt

Woods of Error   Bandits -
                      Torquil

Dream   Giants House
                      Medieval -

Giant

Srambled Senses - Rotunda

emerge from crack into lobby-rotunda of
Escher - stairs - arches - newel posts
with round balls -
Hoggle-bounce ball - wrong way -
  mirror image - can throw ball
    thru mirror
  white marble
  find way out - ball goes thru
  impossible line of set - Taya
    Yollow
  part of set on centrifuge - hoggle
    runs over + around

Garden

high wall - stone -
flowers - fountain - view of Jareth's tower
   birds singing
sunny moment of pause -

↓
thru window

three arches - & exit -

pond - 5 stepping stones - center one sinks

- into hedge maze

some walls - ivy covered

not big deal - go into blind alley
Hoggle waiting for her -

into -

Courtyard —

statue — — 4 large bolted doors
rhythme about whats behind each
Taya impatient — stomps foot to
open — swept — sucked into
down stairs — cellar — mossy
smelly lands in gook — Cess P
slimy creatures ———————
tries to retrace steps — GO TO CASTLE

[CASTLE]

Jareth playing boring game
makes moves — w/ gesture
creature loses — goes up in flames
Jareth picks up weapon — walks
across floor pretends fall + yell
one guy looks around — Jareth sh
pick your poison — guy picks game
begins — bird arrives — 2 mount up
or realizes her lost — runs — Jareth destro

the PITS

looking where door was - Hoggle
pick up lgtern - strange creatures
mouth doorway - slams behind -
moan - LUDO
 save Ludo - Beast comes
they battle Beast - just in time Ludo
grabs Beast throws him in trap -
they go on - Ludo following but they
don't know it - up circular stairs
Ludo panting behind + reveal ?
 Ludo raises stone slab

ISLAND

 Island person - female
haven - food - sleep? Hoggle takes
boat - Taya wakes panic - Hoggle
returns - they depart in boat -
gets dark into canals - Taya makes
decision - into glassy canals
into vertical water
 into

MORE FROM
ARCHAIA AND THE JIM HENSON COMPANY

The Dark Crystal: Creation Myths
Brian Froud, Brian Holguin, Joshua Dysart,
Alex Sheikman, Lizzy John

The Power of the Dark Crystal
Simon Spurrier, Phillip Kennedy Johnson,
Kelly and Nichole Matthews

The Dark Crystal Tales
Cory Godbey

Fraggle Rock: Omnibus
Jeffrey Brown, Katie Cook, Cory Godbey,
Jeff Stokely, and More

Labyrinth: Coronation
Simon Spurrier, Daniel Bayliss, Dan Jackson

Labyrinth Tales
Cory Godbey

The Storyteller
Witches, Dragons, Giants, Fairies
Jeff Stokely, Daniel Bayliss, Conor Nolan,
Tyler Jenkins, and More

The Musical Monsters of Turkey Hollow
The Lost Television Special by Jim Henson and Jerry Juhl
Adapted by Roger Langridge

Jim Henson's Tale of Sand
The Lost Screenplay by Jim Henson and Jerry Juhl
As realized by Ramón K. Pérez